ALIEN OUTBREAK

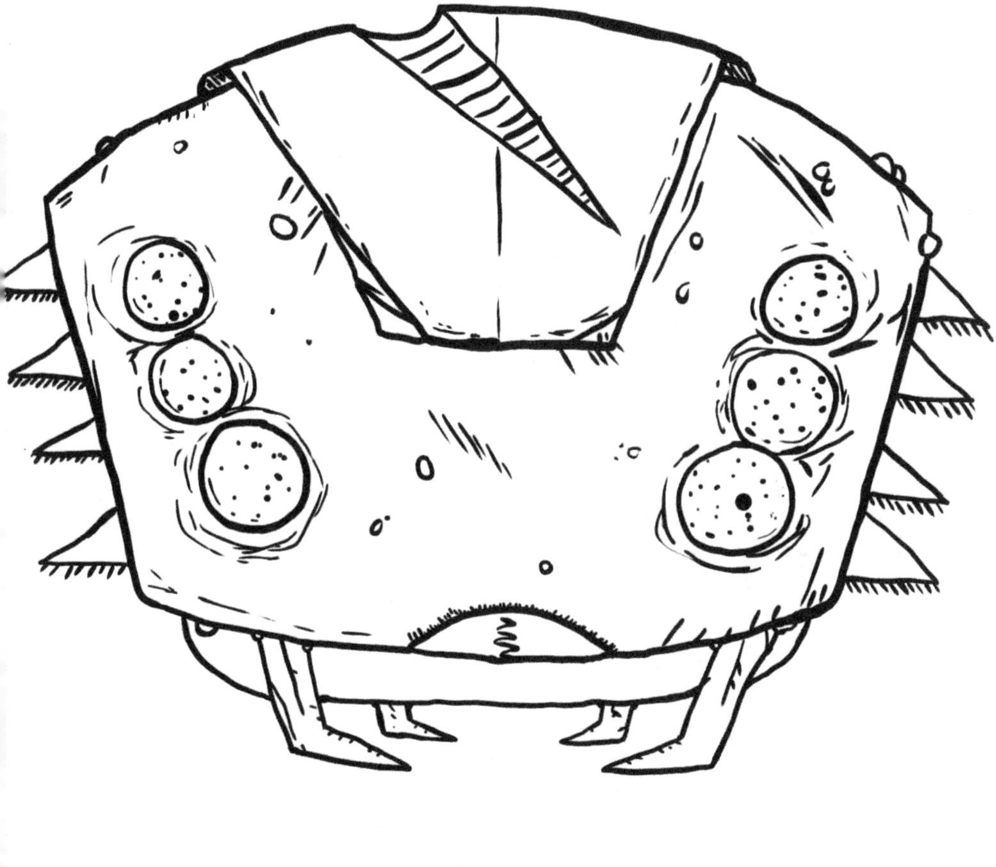

This is a work of fiction. All names, characters, places and incidents are either the product of the author's imagination or are used fictitiously. Any resemblance to actual persons, living or dead, events, or locales is entirely coincidental.

Copyright [symbol] James Bezecny, 2019

All rights reserved. No part of this book may be reproduced in any manner without written permission of the copyright owner except for the use of quotations in a book review.

First paperback edition March 2019

Book design, contents and illustrations by James Bezecny

Published by Pure Venom
https://twitter.com/PureVenomComic

When I started working on what later became Alien Outbreak it wasn't supposed to be anything but a small game to play once or twice with my close friends. I had done a few other tries at making a tabletop game, but those were mostly thought experiments to see what a game would look like if it was based around some odd mechanic or concept. With Alien Outbreak, I wanted to make something that people might actually want to play. For something like that I realized I had pretty much two options: make the game rules loose and open ended, or create some sort of gimmick that would improve replay-ability. Since I've always been kind of a rules jockey I decided on the later and turned to rogue-like video games for inspiration. Because they are designed to be picked up and played they had to be relatively simple but also allow for depth and most of the replay-ability comes from how each play through is unique and difficult. Difficulty has never really been too much of a factor in tabletop games because the game is run by your friend who is sitting at the same table as you, but I figured that if I removed the idea of a "campaign" and focused on individual sessions that killing off characters and wiping the party wouldn't be as big of a deal. At this point, aliens still weren't involved and the game was still floating around as an abstract concept. The aliens were almost slasher-killers, but that turned out to not have enough variety between them so I started throwing together a bunch of traits from real-world animals and monster movies to make something that the players would be scared to face and the rest came from that. Secrecy on the GM side also came about at this point. I wanted to avoid a problem I had run into in my many years of playing D&D 3.5 and Pathfinder; the players knowing exactly what the monsters you are fighting should be capable of. If you play any game long enough, including this one in the long run, you'll start to get a feel for what the monsters can or can't do and by keeping as much of that hidden behind the curtains of a separate set of rules for the aliens, as well as the alien being generated fresh for each session, is there to stave this off for as long as possible and keep the players on their toes.

Table of Contents:

Introduction - pg 1

Part 1: Player's Guide - pg 2
Chapter 1: The Basics - pg 3
Chapter 2: Character Creation - pg 6
Chapter 3: The Rules - pg 14
Chapter 4: Examples of Play - pg 25
Player's Glossary - pg 35

Part 2: Game Master's Guide - pg 38
Chapter 5: The Alien - pg 40
Chapter 6: The Scenario - pg 68
Chapter 7: The Structure of the Game - pg 78

Part 3: Samples and Ready-Mades - pg 84
Chapter 8: Sample Aliens - pg 85
Chapter 9: Sample Scenarios - pg 120
Chapter 10: Sample Worlds - pg 134

Game Master's Glossary - pg 141

Introduction:

So what is Alien Outbreak? Most abstractly, it is a set of guidelines intended to bring a similar experience that one would get from watching a movie like Ridley Scott's "Alien" or John Carpenter's "The Thing." A fear of something that you know almost nothing about aside from that it wants you dead. In more grounded terms, it is a game about half way between a board game and a tabletop role-playing game for 4-8 people that takes about 2-3 hours. That timeframe includes character creation for the players, but the game master may need more time to prepare since they generally have more to keep track of. The game uses procedural generation as a starting point for creating both a scenario of why the players are where they are and what they are doing, and for generating a dangerous alien life-form that will be the "villain" of the game. Each of these variables changes each game in order to create unique and exciting experience.

Since the game is so heavily focused on the unknown aspects of what the alien is, it is important to note here that, **UNLESS YOU ARE PLANNING TO BE THE GAME MASTER, DO NOT READ THE GAME MASTER'S SECTION OR BEYOND.** As a group of players plays more sessions they will start to pick up on bits and pieces of how the "behind the curtain" mechanics work, but intentionally popping the hood and looking at the guts of how the alien and setting work makes the alien a lot less alien and generally kind of kills the fun of things.

PART 1:
Player's Guide

CHAPTER 1: The Basics

The Nitty Gritty:
The basis of this game, as well as any other of it's type, is a form of cooperative storytelling. All of the people playing the game, aside from one player designated as the Game Master (usually shortened to GM), are acting out characters in this story while the GM provides the setting and scenario. If it makes sense for your character to do something, you just tell the GM that you are doing that thing and, unless there is a reason why your character couldn't do that thing, the action your character takes happens in the story. To provide challenge and to keep things interesting, actions in which failure would impact the story require you to roll dice and compare the roll to a desired result. Normally, this type of game isn't about a particular player beating the others and winning, but more about the players as a group overcoming whatever challenges the GM has prepared for them. Alien Outbreak is a bit different in this regard, both in that it is contained in a much shorter scope than most tabletop RPGs (spanning a single 2-3 hour session instead of multiple sessions of 3-5 hours) and in the idea that there is a direct and stated win condition for the players. As with any game that is directly win-able you can also lose, which is one of the reasons that the game is considerably shorter and more self-contained that many other tabletop RPGs.

Alien Outbreak is designed to be fairly quick for new players to pick up and play and the more you play the game the less time you will have to spend on the pre-game set up such as character creation. To play the game you will need a set of polyhedral dice (available at most gaming stores or online) containing a four-sided die, a six-sided die, an eight-sided die, at least one ten-sided die (though having multiple of these makes character creation go a lot quicker) and a 12-sided die, at least one sheet of paper and a pencil per player, a ruler, and a few tokens of some sort to represent the location of the players. (quarters work fine if you don't have anything better, just make sure you can differentiate between each one.)

Playing Alien Outbreak:

If you are reading this book, your job in the game is to take the role of one of the unfortunate folks who will be in the scenario that the GM generates. This could be any type of person, from a highly trained soldier to a civilian who just happened to be in the wrong place at the wrong time, or anything in between. Making a character is pretty easy and should only take about 30 minutes if you are still learning the rules and as few as 10 minutes if you have played a couple times. If this is your first time playing either the GM or an experienced player can help you through the process. Otherwise, the rules for character creation are provided at a later segment of this book is fairly plain language.

This game is designed to be difficult to win and it is very easy for player characters to be killed. If your character dies don't get too hung up on it, Alien Outbreak is a short game and you can try again next time you play. It is also worth noting that the GM is not "out to get you," their job is to make sure the game functions and that it's fun. If there is a problem, such as getting killed in one hit at the start of multiple sessions without a chance to do anything, talk to them about it and try to work out a peaceful situation. If your GM is actually out to get you, they are not doing their job properly.

Another thing to keep in mind with this game is that the alien does not follow the same rules as the players. This is done in order to help the alien "feel more alien" since you don't know exactly what it is capable of, both as in what it's abilities are as well as what it can do from a mechanical/rules standpoint, until you have encountered it a couple times. This may seem unfair. It is, but the game is balanced around that unfairness. While the alien is powerful, there are very few situations where it is impossible to overcome and the mystery and unfairness are mainly there to keep the players on edge rather than to create a mechanically powerful creature.

Dice Notation:

The notation for die rolls used in this book is fairly standard with how other games of the same type note things. Die rolls are listed as XdY+/-Z. X is the number of dice of that type rolled, d is a spacer that stands for "dice" or "die," Y is the number of faces on the die, and Z is any flat numeric modifier. As a whole, it can remembered by thinking of it as "roll X dice with Y faces and add or subtract Z." 3d10+5 calls for a roll of 3 10-sided dice with 5 added. There can also be more complex combinations such as 1d8+2d6-2, which would be for a roll of 1 8-sided die, 2 6-sided dice and subtract 2 from the total.

CHAPTER 2: Character Creation

Creating A Character:
The first thing to do when creating a character is to have a general idea of what type of character you would like to play. Feel free to lean into sci-fi genre conventions and tropes if you don't know where to start. The character you make will only last for a few hours, so you don't need to worry too much about the details of their inner life and you can always play a different type of character next time. This is a role-playing game, but it leans more to the "game" part of that than it does to the "roleplaying" part.

It's also not a bad idea to coordinate with the other players on what characters everyone playing. While Alien Outbreak is possible to win with any combination of character types, covering a wide variety of skills and abilities ensures that everyone is bringing something unique to the table and people aren't competing to make "the better" of the same character. This also makes the game easier as it means that there are more options that the players as a group have access to. It is recommended that you have a group of at least one scientist, one engineer, and at least half the group as soldiers if you want to have the easiest time. All of this is just recommendation however, and a group of all scientists or civilians can be just as formidable a team.

Statistics:
Once you have a general idea of what type of character you want to play, roll 12d10. If you feel like you rolled exceptionally low, total up the value of all the dice you rolled. If the total is less than 50, you can re-roll the lowest dice until the total is at least 50. Then arrange these into 6 groups of 1-3 dice. Then assign each group to one of the following statistics:
- **Strength** - Your physical strength, determines how much you can carry and increases melee damage you deal by

1/2 the score.
- **Toughness** - How much of a beating you can take, decreases as you take damage (this damage can be restored, but only to your original toughness). If you run out of toughness, you die.
- **Perception** - Used for noticing details and finding things
- **Intelligence** - A measure of how much knowledge you have. Determines how many skill points you get.
- **Agility** - Determines how hard you are to hit and is used for activities that require quick movement.
- **Morale** - How much stress you can deal with, decreases when thing go poorly (this can be restored and can go above your original morale). If you run out of morale, you panic and are limited in what actions you can take.

It is recommended that each statistic has at 2 dice going towards it since a balanced character generally has more survivability.

Alternative Rolling Methods:
There are a variety of reasons that you may not want to roll 12d10 all at once. Below are a number of methods for determining statistics that do not require a large number of dice:

Method One: Roll 2d10 and record the number, do this 6 times keeping the results seperate. Assign each result to a statistic of your choice, only applying one result per statistic.

Method Two: You start with 12 points. Spend 1-3 points per statistic, then roll a number of dice equal to the number of points you spent on each statistic. Each result is the value of that statistic.

Method Three: You start with 6 points. Roll 1d10 6 times and record each result seperately. Assign each result to a seperate statistic. You may then spend up to 2 points per statistic to add 1d10 per point spent to the value of that statistic.

Method Four: As a group, roll 1d10 12 times and have each person record each die result seperately. Each person can then assign 1-3 of those results to statistics of their choice.

Method Five: As a group, roll 2d10 6 times and have each person record each result sperately. Each person may then assign each result to a statistic.

Kits:

Next, you must pick a kit. Kits are a short hand for the general archetype your character follows. They provide bonuses to some of your statistics, determine which skills you can put points into, and provide some basic equipment for your character. Kits are just a general concept and you should pick whichever you feel works best for what you want to play rather than what the name is. For example, the "soldier" kit could be a whole host of things: actual member of the military, a violent criminal, a paranoid survivalist, etc.

- **Civilian:**
   Statistic Bonus: +5 to any one statistic
   Skills: Climb, Swim, Drive, Pilot, Stealth, Social
- Additionally, a civilian picks 3 skills from the other classes and can put ranks in those skills as well.
   Equipment: pick 2 general items, pick 1 item from another kit
- **Engineer:**
   Statistic Bonus: +5 perception and intelligence
   Skills: Electrical, Mechanical, Explosive, Jury Rig, Climb, Swim, Drive, Pilot, Stealth, Social
   Equipment: Tool Kit, Vehicle Key, pick 1 general item
- **Scientist:**
   Statistic Bonus: +10 intelligence
   Skills: Biology, Chemistry, Surgery, Theoretical Science, Climb, Swim, Drive, Pilot, Stealth, Social
   Equipment: Medical Kit, Specimen Bag, pick 1 general item
- **Soldier:**
   Statistic Bonus: +5 strength and agility
   Skills: Melee Combat, Firearms, Explosives, Survival, Climb, Swim, Drive, Pilot, Stealth, Social
   Equipment: Body Armor, pick 1 weapon, pick 1 general item

Androids:

Humans are the default for what your character will be, but there is also the option to play as an android. Androids get the following modifications:
- +5 to strength and intelligence.
- Cannot take morale damage or increase morale.
- Cannot heal or be healed through medical kits or medicine. The only way to heal an android is to have another character use the jury rig skill, which heals the same amount as regular healing would to a human.
- Androids do not have vitals, but do generate heat.
- Each time you take 5 or more damage you must roll a toughness check or you lose a limb. The GM decides which limb you lose and this can include your head. If your head is removed you do not die, but cannot see. If an arm is removed you lose 5 strength. If a leg is lost you can only move at 15' per action and lose 5 agility.
- You cannot take any knowingly hostile actions against humans, even in self-defense.

It is recommended to keep the amount of androids in the party to a minimum, both for theming and because a majority of the group having the limitations of an android can lead to some severe hinderances in many scenarios..

Skill Points:

Then you must assign skill points. You get a number of skill points equal to 10 + your intelligence which you can put into any of the skills you got from your kit. You can put up to 15 skill points into a single skill. Skills can also be learned in session. When some-one fails at a skill check that is not repeatable, they get +1 to the skill. You can only increase a skill to twice of how many skill points they put in it at character creation. The specifics of what each skill does are listed in Chapter 3: The Rules.

Equipment:

Next is equipment. Most of your equipment is given to you by your class, but you also get 1 general item (unless you are a civilian, in which case you get 2) from the list below:

- **Acid:** Can melt through solid objects other than glass. If spilled it deals 1d4 damage and the victim must make an agility check or the take the damage again the next round. Can be made with chemistry.
- **Adrenaline:** When consumed, increases toughness by 10 and strength by 5 for an hour, after which the toughness and strength bonuses are lost. Can be made with chemistry.
- **Anti-Toxin:** Cures a specific ailment when consumed. Can be made with medicine, but must be made for a specific ailment that must be properly studied beforehand. If you have not encountered a specific uncommon or alien ailment you cannot make an anti-toxin for it.
- **Backpack:** Can carry an additional 2 items. Does not count as an item when determining how much you can carry.
- **Bandages:** when consumed it restores 5 toughness. Can be made with medicine.
- **Batteries:** Restores power to an item powered by electricity or some other power source.
- **Binoculars:** Grants +5 on perception checks to see things at a distance.
- **Camera:** Can take pictures or video, might have a flash.
- **Climbing Gear:** Can climb at 20' per round. Can be made with mechanical.
- **Flashlight:** Provides 30' light, has enough power to last an hour. Can be made with mechanical.
- **Knife:** A melee weapon dealing 1d4+2+1/2 your strength in damage.
- **Motion Sensor:** Makes noise when some-thing moves within 15' of it. Can be made with electrical.
- **Pain Suppressers:** When consumed it increases toughness by 15 to a maximum of your initial toughness for an hour. Can be made with medicine.

- **Pistol:** A small handgun with 40' range, 7 shot clip and deals 1d8 damage.
- **Poison:** When consumed a toughness check must be made or the consumer take 1d3 damage each round until they make a toughness check. They get a new toughness check each round. Can be made with chemistry.
- **Scuba Gear:** Allows the user to hold breath indefinitely.
- **Snacks:** Restores 1d4 morale when consumed.
- **Sound Recorder/Player:** Can record and play sounds, might have music on it.
- **Space Suit:** Wearer can act in space and does not take damage from space or vacuums.
- **Trap:** If walked into it entangles the target if they fail an agility check, denying them movement until they take an action to make an agility check to escape. Can be made with mechanical.
- **Walkie Talkie/Radio:** Can communicate with other people with this item. Can be made with electrical.

Listed below are the specifics of items granted by classes:
- **Body Armor:** Has 10 toughness which takes damage instead of you until it has no more toughness at which point it is destroyed. Can be repaired through mechanical or jury rig.
- **Bomb:** Deals 3d6 to all within 10' when detonated, 2d6 to all within 20' and 1d6 to all within 30'. Can be set up with a remote detonator or a timer.
- **Firearms:**
  - **Flame Thrower:** 25' range, 3 "shot" clip, deals 3d6 damage, comes with 2 clips, if there is a flammable object

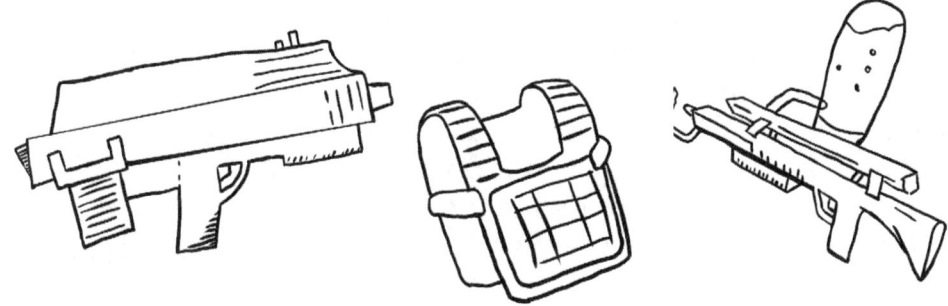

or creature adjacent to the target it must make an agility check or take 1d6 damage.
- **Light Machine Gun:** 80' range, 7 shot clip, deals 2d6 damage, comes with 3 clips, counts as 2 items for carrying it.
- **Machine Gun:** 80' range, 5 shot clip, deals 1d8 damage, comes with 3 clips.
- **Rifle:** 160' range, 5 shot clip, deals 1d10 damage, comes with 3 clips.
- **Rocket Launcher:** 120' range, 1 shot "clip", comes with 2 clips, deals 6d6 to all within 5' when detonated, 4d6 to all within 10' and 2d6 to all within 15'.
- **Shotgun:** 40' range, 4 shot clip, deals 2d6 damage, comes with 3 clips.
- **Medical Kit:** When used grants +3 on skill totals for surgery checks, can be used 3 times.
- **Melee Weapon:** Deals 1d6+1/2 your strength in damage.
- **Specimen Bag:** Safely contains any biohazards inside and comes with the equipment to procure specimens and take samples. Has 1 cage that can fit a tiny alien.
- **Tool Kit:** Applies to either mechanical or electrical. Increases your effective skill to the type of check that it applies to by 3.
- **Vehicle Key:** Connects to a specific vehicle (usually the ship you flew in on) provided by the GM and allows control of that vehicle.

Vehicles:

Vehicles only require skill checks to operate when used for fancy and dangerous maneuvers. You may or may not need a vehicle key to operate. When using a vehicle your agility is reduced and you cannot must take an action each turn to control the vehicle. Maneuvering vehicles is typically modified by agility. Vehicles have their own movements speeds as well as their own toughness. Using a vehicle that is below half it's toughness takes a -5 penalty to your skill total. When a vehicle reaches 0 toughness it is destroyed and can no longer operate.

Here are some example vehicles:
- **Land Rover:** A small buggy car that can hold 4. 75toughness, -5 agility, 120' speed.
- **Power Lifter:** A humanoid armature for lifting crates and other heavy loads. 75 toughness, -10 agility, 20' speed.
- **Helicopter:** A flying ship that can't leave orbit with space for 3 people. 150 toughness, -10 agility, 120' flight speed.
- **Transport Ship:** A standard space transport ship with space for up to 50 passengers. 300 toughness, -15 agility, 90' flight speed.
- **Mining Drill:** A large drill designed for cutting through metals and rocks. Piloted by a single person. 150 toughness, -15 agility, 15' speed.
- **Cargo Ship:** A compact spacecraft primarily composed of cargo space. Can support up to 10 people.

Statistic Bonuses:

Lastly there is a bit of book keeping to note on your sheet. Next to each statistic, note 1/2 it's total. This is called the "statistic bonus" and is the value you add to skill checks that use that attribute. This is not always the same attribute for the same skill, you might add your perception bonus to a electrical skill check to identify a problem, but intelligence to fix the problem. Attacking skills always key off of agility. You should also note how many items you can carry at one time. You can carry 2 items, plus 1 additional item per 3 points of strength above 6.

And that's it!

Once all the players at the table have created characters and the GM has set up the scenario and alien you are ready to play! There is an example of this process in action in Chapter Four: Examples of Play.

CHAPTER 3: The Rules

Taking Actions:
In general, you can have your character do whatever a person in their situation would be able to do. If you want to do something that has a significant effect if you were to fail at it, such as shooting at an alien or repairing a generator quickly, you will have to roll a skill check.

Skill Checks:
Skill checks are done by adding your score in the appropriate skill with the appropriate statistic bonus added to it. Then roll 3d10 and compare the result of the roll to your skill total. If your roll is lower than the skill total, you have succeeded. A roll result of 3-5 is an automatic success and a roll result of 30 is always a failure. Some rolls, such as attacking rolls or piloting a heavily damaged vehicle, may cause a penalty to your skill total. The GM will tell you how much of a penalty this is.

Statistic Checks:
A GM can also call for a "statistic check." This is done by rolling 3d10 and comparing the result to the statistic the GM tells to roll for. If it is less than statistic, you succeed.

Combat:
Out of combat, there are no specific "turns" and players are free to do as they wish. In combat however, your actions are much more streamlined and ordered. Combat is broken into "rounds" and "turns." A round is the sum of all the individual turns, each character in the combat getting one turn per round. The alien does not always follow this, but generally gets it's turn before everyone unless it is ambushed in some fashion. Turn order is otherwise decided upon by the players, who can choose when they act in relation to each other. On your turn you get one action. This action can be used for one of the following actions:

- Move up to 30'
- Climb or swim up to 10'
- Run up to 60' (this causes you to take 1 damage)
- Interact with something (open a door, pick up a box, draw a weapon, reload a weapon, etc)
- Stand up from prone
- Attack a foe (either a foe next to you for melee or within the weapon's range for firearms)
- Various other actions as subject to GM discretion

If you take an action that does not cause you to move and you are standing, you can move 5' before or after you take your action.

The Combat Map:

Combat often references specific distances in 5' increments. For this reason it is recommended, but not required, that each player has a token of some sort to represent their character's location in a fight. All the tokens should be of about the same size and that size becomes the scale. One token width is 5' of distance. The alien may be larger or smaller and a proportionally sized token should be used to represent this. It works best when the tokens are 1" across. These tokens are to be placed on some sort of representation of the space where combat takes place with notation for where walls, doors, tables, etc are. Generally, it is not necessary for the GM to create a fully drawn out map in advanced, but they may want to consider it if there is a particularly complex set-piece where they anticipate combat.

Taking Damage:

If you are hit by a physical attack, or if the GM tells you, you take
damage. The GM will tell you how much. This reduces your toughness by the amount of damage taken, but damage can generally be healed, but this takes a successful medicine or surgery check as covered in the skill rules. If you take

damage in combat, you take a penalty equal to the amount of damage you took for the rest of the current round. If you took damage after you have taken your turn for the current round, you take that penalty until the end of the next round.

Dying:
If you reach 0 toughness, you die. When a player character dies they aren't entirely out of the game. Near the end of the game, there is the reveal of a dynamic difficulty score that the GM has been tracking throughout the game that the players will be able to use to influence the game. Any players with dead characters are the people who make the choices on how this score is used, and it is possible to use this to bring a character back to life.

Morale Damage:
If you take damage by a mental attack, or if something horrific happens, you take morale damage. The GM will tell you when this happens and how much, but here is a general list of things that cause morale damage:
- When you have to run from the alien you lose 1 morale.
- When you see a human die or abandon a human to die you must make a morale check or lose 1d4 morale.
- When you encounter the alien for the first time you must make a morale check or lose 1d4 morale.

Similar to regular damage, this damage decreases your morale and you take penalties the same as if you had taken regular damage. Morale can be regained, but it is more difficult to do so that to recover from regular damage. You can regain 1 morale when you succeed at a significant and non-repeatable skill check or 1d4 if you kill an alien. Like toughness, you cannot exceed your initial morale through gaining morale.

Panic:
If you reach 0 morale you fall into a panic. While in this state, you automatically fail all skill checks but can move at 40' instead of 30' and run at 80' instead of 60'. A panic lasts

until you have reached safety and remain there for about 5 minutes, at which point you can make a check against your original morale. If you succeed you regain 1d4 morale. If you fail you can retry the check 10 minutes later.

Skills:
Each skill has a particular use as described below:
- **Biology:** Used to identify biological substances and analyze creatures. It takes an hour to attempt to identify a single thing or analyze a single feature of a creature if you have a sample. If you do not have a sample it you can only theorize about what you are trying to figure out; this takes 30 minutes and you only use 1/2 the skill total.
- **Chemistry:** Used to make chemical compounds including medicines, as well as to identify acids and other chemicals. Making medicine takes 1 hour assuming that you know what how to make what you are making and 1d3+1 hours if you do not.
- **Climb:** Used to move on a vertical surface. Only needs to be rolled in non-ideal circumstances, such as a slime covered wall or the like.
- **Drive:** Used to drive a ground vehicle. Only needs to be rolled in non-ideal circumstances, such as shaking off an alien clinging to the vehicle.
- **Electrical:** Used to repair computers or circuitry and make uses of them. Takes a minimum of 30 minutes.
- **Explosives:** Used to make and handle explosives. It takes an hour to make an explosive and 1d4 rounds to handle an explosive. Handling explosives covers planting them, disarming them and the like. Every part of the explosive building and planting them is considered dangerous for if it requires a check or not.
- **Firearms:** Used to make attacks with firearms.
- **Jury Rig:** Used to make odd things or things from spare parts. Also used to repair androids and for situations involving alien technology.
- **Mechanical:** Used to repair mechanical devices. Takes a minimum of 30 minutes.
- **Melee:** Used to make melee attacks. Melee attacks deal 1d4+1/2 your strength if unarmed, or by equipment.
- **Pilot:** Used to drive a air, space or water vehicle. Otherwise functions as drive.
- **Social:** Used to influence people in any way.

- **Stealth:** Used to remain hidden or hide. It gets a penalty equal to 1/2 the perception score of those who are looking for you. Unlike other skills, the GM rolls stealth for you and does not need to tell you the result.
- **Surgery:** Used to perform medical operations from first aid to brain surgery. In addition to autopsies and the like, you can use this skill to heal someone takes 1 minute and yields 1d4 toughness recovered. For every 5 that you succeed at the check by the person recovers an additional point of toughness. You cannot use surgery on yourself.
- **Survival:** Used to create shelter, find food and and track creatures.
- **Swim:** Used to swim. Only needs to be rolled in non-ideal circumstances, such as for getting out of a whirlpool.
- **Theoretical Science:** Used when chemistry and biology do not apply or for situations where the science of mankind either does not understand or does not apply.

Improving Skills:
Skills can be improved throughout the game. If you fail a skill check that is significant and/or non-repeatable you get +1 to skill totals with that skill. This can happen a number of times for each skill equal to how many skill points you put into that skill at character creation.

The Dynamic Difficulty Score:
During the second act, the GM keeps track of a score meant to measure how much trouble the players have run into or how well they have been doing. This score is hidden from the players until it is revealed at the start of the third act. The score goes up when bad things happen to the players or down when the players do well.

At the start of the third act, the players must spend the dynamic difficulty score either down to 0 or up to 0. If the score is positive, the options they have to pick from are good for them. If the score is negative, the options they have to pick from are bad for them. In the event that there are dead player characters, those players have a monopoly on how the score is spent.

Dynamic Difficulty Options:
You cannot select the same option multiple times unless the option says otherwise.

These options are also listed in the Game Master's section of this book with different framing and levels of detail required for executing the selected option, but the rules on how the score is calculated are only in this book.

Positive Score:
- **3pts** - A dead player character managed to survive after all! They were probably hiding in the vents or something.
- **2pts** - A dead non-player character managed to survive after all! This functions the same as bringing back a player, but the GM has more control of it.
- **2pts** - There is a hidden weapons cache in the facility!
- **2pts** - One of the remaining scientist NPCs, or a scientist player, thinks they have a way to create a virus that specifically targets alien biology. When the virus is finished, it can be dispersed through the facilities vents or sewers or some-thing. This cannot be selected if there are no scientists. If there are no vents or sewers, a dispersal unit can be built by an engineer. If there are no vents, sewers or engineers some-one will have to inject it into the alien or inject it into a person and have that person get eaten.
- **1pts** - Outside help is on the way!
- **1pts** - The alien's weakness is revealed! If the alien has a weakness the GM tells you what it is, otherwise the GM tells you what it's weakest attribute is.
- **1pts** - A player who was injured by the alien starts displaying the traits of the alien (if they were dead they come back to life). The alien is drawn to this player for the final confrontation.

- **1pts** - Someone found something! A player gets one item of their choice from the general items list or their class items list. You can select this option multiple times.
- **1pts** - The players get a second wind! Each player regains 1d4 toughness. A player can opt out to grant someone else their 1d4 of healing, but any given player can only regain 2d4 toughness from this option.
- **1pts** - Someone learned something! A player gains +1d4 to a skill of their choice. This option can be selected multiple times but only once per player.

Negative Score:
- **4pts** - Another type of alien shows up! Oh Boy! This one requires a pause in the game while the GM creates the new alien.
- **3pts** - The alien has reproduced.. Some how.
- **2pts** - Those killed by the alien come back to life under the control of the alien.
- **2pts** - The alien is converting the area into some-thing more suitable to it.
- **2pts** - The alien is too dangerous to escape, one of the NPCs is found to have destroyed all the exits, ways out, and communication with the outside world to seal the alien in.
- **1pts** - Destruction! Part of the facility is destroyed and inaccessible.
- **1pts** - Power trouble! The power in the facility goes out. The backup power needs to be activated manually in an appropriate room with either a mechanical or electrical check depending on the nature of the damage.
- **1pts** - A storm is brewing. In a bit, a massive storm will hit. Being outside in the storm deals damage each round. While inside, power loss in certain rooms may occur, certain rooms may collapse and it is loud.
- **1pts** - A player who was injured or killed by the alien starts displaying the traits of the alien (if they were dead they come back to life). If they were killed by the alien, that player still controls them but they are working

- with the alien now.
- **1pts** - Outside forces (government, "the company", etc) have decided to nuke the whole place from afar. The players are tasked with containing the alien so it gets killed in the blast.

Environmental Rules:

Not everything that happens outside of your control is hidden under the Game Master's section. Those things are covered here.

Acid: If you are splashed with acid you take 1d4 damage. Having most of your body coated in acid from something like falling into a vat of it or having it poured on you instead deals 15 damage.

Collapse: If a wall, rocks, a building or whatever else falls on you it knocks you prone and you take either 4, 8, 12 or 24 damage at the GM's option.

Cold: If you are caught in cold weather for prolonged amounts or time or are exposed to exreme cold you take 1 damage on a round by round or minute by minute basis depending on the nature of the situation.

Darkness: When in darkness you can't make out details, may not be allowed to know what is in the area, and take a -5 to all skill totals. You are also more likely to be surprised.

Falling: If you fall from a height of 10' or more, you take 4 damage per 10' fallen. Additionally, any time you take damage from falling you fall prone.

Fire: Passing through fire deals 2 damage per 5' passed through. If you are on fire you take 4 damage per round and must take an action to make an agility check in order to put yourself out. This damage bypasses body armor.

Jumping: You can roll an ability check to jump. You jump a number of feet across equal to twice the amount you made the check by, and up the amount you made the check by. You have a minimum distance of 1/5 your agility in feet across and 1/10 your agility up. If you failed the check, you jump the minimum distance.

Radiation: Being exposed to radiation deals 1 damage per minute. After the exposure ends you continue to take damage for 2d6 more minutes.

Smoke: Smoke blocks line of sight and forces you to hold your breath as if you were underwater or you can only take actions to move and you move at 1/2 speed.

Underwater: You can hold your breath for 1 round per 1/5 your toughness + 1 per skill rank in swimming, after this passes you take 2 damage per round submersed. This damage bypasses body armor.

Vacuum of Space: If you are directly and suddenly exposed to the vacuum of space, you die immediately. In the case of rapid depressurization it instead deals 1d4 damage per round, increasing by 1 damage for each further round. This damage bypasses body armor.

Continued Play:
While Alien Outbreak is designed for single session play with new characters each time, if a player character survives a game that player is free to use that character in future games with a few modifications:
- They can only take 3 items from the previous game with them.
- Any skill increases gained in previous games count as the base score for the purpose of further improvement. The maximum a skill can get to on any character at any time is 30.
- Any losses to statistics are removed unless they were

caused by an effect that specifically says that those losses cannot be regained.

CHAPTER 4: Examples of Play

This section is designed to provide a "sample" of how aspects of the game work and show examples of some of the mechanics which have already been explained in this book with the intention of clarifying anything that is unclear.

Example Gameplay:
The year is 2264. Humans have expanded out to other worlds but it is almost entire for mining or other resource gathering purposes. Faster than light travel has been invented but because of how much power it consumes it is usually one way and only used for emergency response. Otherwise, space travel takes very long and the travelers have to be put into suspended
animation in order to survive the journey. The players have been sent by Hopkins and Oslin Astro-Mining to the Hopkins and Oslin Gravium Mine on CS-264, commonly called the "Hopkins Humanitarian Charity Mine," because the workers there complained about an unknown creature that eats the rare alloy. The job the players are tasked with is to enter the facility to eliminate these creatures, assess profitability of the facility and, if the facility is found to be no longer profitable, liquidate all employees with extreme
prejudice. So far they have been given the lay of the land and the head
scientist, Nigil Brant, has shown them the dead specimen and told them what they know about these strange creatures.

GM: "The creature is in a glass jar and appears to be some kind of
cat-sized inky black lump with a number of small eyes covering the main mass. Four multi-jointed legs extend down from the body and just seem to end in stumps. A large chunk of it has been blown off by gunfire Nigil

informs you that one of the security people shot this one which had
managed to make it's way into the store room, but that the miners have seen others scurrying around down in the mine. They haven't attacked anyone yet, but hiss when people try to approach."

Ben: "Well, my character is a scientist so I'm going to perform an autopsy."

GM: "Okay, that'll take about an hour. Roll either a surgery check or
theoretical science check, modified by perception since you are looking for details."

Ben: "I'll use theoretical, since I put more points into that. I've got 10 points in that and my intelligence is 18, so the total is 19."
Rolls dice and gets a 13.
"Alright, I made it. What do I find out?"

GM: "Before I get to that, is there anything that anyone else wants to do in hour it's going to take him to do the autopsy?"

Sean: "Yeah, I want to check out the mineshaft and see what kind of place we're dealing with here."

Armand: "I'll go with him in case we get attacked by anything while we're down there."

GM: "Do you want to do anything Sally?"

Sally: "Is there a security system I can take a look at? If one of these things got into the storeroom, I want to see how it got there without people
noticing."

GM: "Sounds good. The security guard, Dennis Silver, leads

you into a security booth. While he's explaining the system and facility to you, we'll go to Sean and Armand. One of the engineers leads you both to an old elevator and tells you that it's the only way in or out of the main mineshaft. Going inside, there are a number of space suit on the walls and the engineer
explains that there isn't any atmosphere in the shaft, so you'll have to wear one."

Armand: "I put on one of the suits."

Sean: "Same here."

GM: "The suits are pretty old and smell like they need to be cleaned, but they should do the job. As you are finishing suiting up, the elevator grinds to a halt quite loudly. The engineer says "Alright, here we are. Just give this old thing a minute to depressurize." A hissing sound starts up and the suits puff up a bit as air is sucked out of the room. After a bit the doors open into a dark space with only a few work-lights scattered around. There is a large mining drill that looks about 60 years out of date hooked up to a generator. It is currently inactive."

Sean: "I pull out my flashlight to get a better look at how big the shaft is."

GM: "The shaft is pretty narrow, about 10' across, but it's long enough where your flashlight doesn't reach the end of it."

Sean: "Alright. I head down the shaft, keeping an eye out for anything
moving."

Armand: "I'll follow and keep a lookout as well. Also, I draw my machine gun."

GM: "Alright, roll perception checks both of you."

Sean: "I've got 12 perception."
Rolls dice
"Ugh. 19. Looks like I failed."

Armand: "Same here."

GM: "The shaft goes down quite a ways and is relatively smooth. There are some holes in the walls, but they look more like pockets in the rock than like tunnels or anything. There are also some obviously man-made diversions from the shaft where there used to be a vein of gravium. After a couple minutes of walking you reach the end of the main shaft. Can I get another perception check from both of you?"

Sean: "Okay, I passed this time."

Armand: "Still failed. Probably wasn't the best idea to have 3 perception."

GM: "Don't worry about it. Before we deal with what Sean's character sees, we'll cut back to Sally."

Sally: "Cool. What's the deal with the security."

GM: "It's pretty spotty as far as camera placement. Dennis explains that a lot of the cameras have broken down over the years and that most of the rooms don't have full coverage. You've reviewed the tapes-"

Sally: "This place uses tapes?"

GM: "My bad, I forgot this is the future. It's obviously on mini-DVDs."

Entire group groans.

GM: "Anyway, you've reviewed the mini-DVDs of the storeroom and the creature pushes it's way in from the door into the main hallway. There isn't a security camera in the hallway though."

Sally: "I check the other rooms in the area at the time before it entered the storeroom."

GM: "Roll perception."

Sally: "I passed."

GM: "Well, you don't see the creature on any other cameras, but you can tell it isn't coming up through the elevator shaft, so it must have another way in."

Sally: "Hmm... I'll have to take a look around in person."

GM: "Meanwhile, back the mineshaft."

Sean: "What do I see?"

GM: "As you turn around to head back, you see a flicker of movement
heading into on of the mined out gravium veins. It was moving pretty fast so you didn't get a good look at it."

Sean: "I check it out. I'm going to try to sneak up on it."

Armand: "Wait, I should do this since you don't have a gun."

Sean: "That makes sense."

GM: Rolls stealth.
"So you creep up to the passage. Since you're sneaking you don't have very good lighting so you are feeling out the passage as you go."

Rolls some dice.
Rolls some more dice.
"...Alright. So you're heading down the passage and all of a sudden you hear something behind you. Before you have a chance to turn around, you feel a sharp pain in your shoulder and you start bleeding heavily. Your suit was torn and it starts rapidly depressurizing."
Rolls some dice.
"You take 6 damage from having a chunk of your shoulder torn out and 3 damage from the depressurization."

Armand: "Yikes. That's a lot. The body armor takes the 6 from the bite, but does the depressuriztion ignore the armor?"

GM: "Yep. Turning around you are face to face with a much larger version of the creature from the lab. Whereas the one you saw there was about two feet tall, this one is eight and has a large beak hanging down from it's torso at about head level. Make a morale check."

Armand: "Phew. Made it. Almost failed because of the damage penalty though."

GM: "You manage to keep your cool. Sean, you hear a chomping sound and Armand yelling in pain from down the passage. We're in combat now, the alien has already had it's turn so which one of you wants to go first?"

Armand: "I want to blast this thing in the face. Sean, you don't have a
weapon so you should probably hang back."

Sean: "Actually I've got a knife, but after seeing how much damage it dealt I don't want anything to do with this thing. You should get out of there so I can fix your suit."

GM: "The alien is right in his path right now."

Armand: "This is looking pretty grim. I move five feet back and unload on this thing."

GM: "Roll firearms at a -3 to your total. Don't forget about your damage penalty either."

Armand: "Good thing I put all my skill points into firearms. I've got 6 from skill points and my agility is 25, so with the penalties I've got to get a 14 or less."
Rolls some dice.
"All ones! I hit! Seven damage."

GM: "That's a pretty solid hit and it's gore sprays onto you, covering the front of your suit. It shrieks in pain, but is still standing. Sean, you hear some gunfire and the most horrific sound in your life. Roll morale."

Sean: "Didn't make it."

GM: "You recognize that whatever made that sound must have been big and it spooks you. You lose 2 morale. It's your turn, what do you want to do?"

Sean: "I'll move into the passage and shine my light."

GM: "You see the creature that Armand has been fighting and it looks like both of them are bleeding pretty badly. Back to the alien's turn; Armand, you take 4 damage from depressurization. The creature lets out another yell and bolts past Armand into the darkness. You could probably use survival to track the blood stains."

Sean: "There are more pressing things here. I'm going to use mechanical and my tool kit to repair the suit."

Armand: "I'm pretty low and probably wouldn't survive the amount of time he needs to repair the suit. Can I put my hand over the tear to slow it down while we get out of the shaft?"

GM: "Sure. I'm going to cut back to Ben since it's been a while. Ben; the autopsy has been very interesting. You've determined that the creature's reproductive organs seem to be either vestigial or severely underdeveloped. They also appear to have a gizzard with gravium dust in it that you think helps them digest hard minerals. There is a small, but hard beak that you are pretty sure they could use to tunnel through solid metal."

Sally: "That's probably how they got in the supply room without using the elevator."

Ben: "Yeah, and given that there was a bigger one down in the mine, they probably grow a lot before they reproduce. Which means there could be a lot of these things running around."

Armand: "Hey Ben, can I get some medical attention here..."

Example Character Creation:
The group has been talking over what each person wants their characters to be. Since it is their first time playing, they are taking the advice to have half
the group play as soldiers. Given the premise that they are all working for a large corporation that has no qualms with killing off employees if it means more profits, Armand has the idea to play as a debtor to that corporation who was given the option for paying off his debt by becoming a "bug-hunter," who is sent into situations where aliens are reported and clean up any messes. After telling this to the GM, he approves it.

Armand starts out by rolling 12d10 and gets results of 6, 2, 6, 5, 5, 10, 6, 2, 1, 1, 7, and 7. He knows he wants to have really high agility since he'll be

making a lot of attack rolls and puts 10, 5 and 5 into it for a total of 20. He also wants a good amount of toughness and strength, so he puts 6, 6, and 1 into toughness for a total of 13 and puts 6 and 7 into strength for a total of 13. He knows that perception is pretty important as well but is running low on, so he puts 7 and 2 into it for a total of 9. While he realizes that morale and intelligence are important, he's running out of dice and values
intelligence over morale, since he needs the skill points for his firearms skill, so he puts 7 into intelligence by itself, leaving 2 and 1 for morale for a total of 3.

From all this, Armand reasons that his character was a skilled laborer before he became a bug-hunter and his low morale is due to years of crushing debt.

Next, Armand picks a kit. While he briefly looks at civilian since it could get him a couple of skills that would relate to his backstory while still being able to get access to the firearms skill, but wants body armor as well as a weapon so he picks soldier. This gives him +5 strength and agility, bringing them up to 25 and 18 respectively. It allows him access to the melee combat, firearms, explosives, survival, climb, swim, drive, pilot, stealth, social skills.
Additionally, he starts with a firearm of his choice, a set of body armor and a general item of his choice.

Armand notes these things and moves on to spending his skill points. His intelligence is 9 so he starts with 19 skill points. He has a high agility already, so he puts 6 points into firearms so that his attack rolls will be against 18. This leaves him with 13 skill points. He then puts 3 points into melee combat since he doesn't want to be defenseless if he runs out of ammunition, puts 3 points into pilot reasoning that he flew commercial ships before becoming a bug-hunter, 2 points into stealth since his character was on the run for a while because of his debts, 2 points into explosives for the fun of it, 1 point into social for flavor and his last point into climb just in case.

Now Armand picks his equipment. Since he is a soldier, he gets to pick a firearm of his choice. Knowing that the group is going into a mine, he picks up a shotgun for the close quarters damage. He notes the 10 toughness his body armor starts with. For his general item he picks climbing gear because he doesn't know about the layout of the mine.

Armand is now done with his character and is ready to play.

Players Glossary:

Acid - Deals damage to a character when submerged or splashed. Page 22

Actions - What a character can do. Page 14

Agility - A statistic that measures how well a character can control their physcial actions. Page 7

Alien - The main antagonist of the game. Page 4

Android - A synthetic humanoid that players can pick as an alternative to being human. Page 9

Civilian - A generalist kit that is weaker but can pick their options. Page 8

Combat - A more heavily metered section of play used for life or death situations. Page 14

Combat Round - A measure of all of the turns for each character once. Page 14

Combat Turn - A single character's actions during a combat round. Page 14

Collapse - What happens when heavy objects fall on a character. Page 22

Cold - Covers exposure to extreme cold. Page 22

Damage - A reduction to toughness as the result of Physical injury taken. Page 15

Death/Dying - A state that occurs when a character reaches 0 toughness. Page 16

Dice Notation - A system of shorthand for how many dice as well as what type to roll. Page 5

Dynamic Difficulty Score - A score kept by the game master that records how well or how poorly the players are doing. Page 20

Engineer - A kit focused on repairing or creating machines. Page 8

Equipment - A collection of carried items. Page 10

Falling - Deals damage when a character falls a long distance. Page 22

Fire - Deals damage to characters when exposed to it. Page 22

Game Master - The person running the alien, scenario and game at large. Page 3
Human - The default option for player characters. Page 9
Intelligence - A statistic that measures a character's knowledge. Page 7
Item - An object that can be owned by a character. Page 10
Jumping - How far a character can leap. Page 22
Kits - A set of equipment, skill options and bonuses to certain statistics. Page 8
Morale - A statistic that measures how well a character can cope with stress and fear. Page 7
Morale Damage - A reduction to morale as the result of fear or other mental injury taken. Page 16
Panic - A state that occurs when a character reaches 0 morale. Page 16
Perception - A statistic that measures how attentive to detail and their surroundings a character is. Page 7
Player - All the people playing the game. Usually seperate from the game master. Page 3
Radiation - Covers the effects of exposure to dangerous radiation. Page 23
Scientist - A kit focused on intelligence and science. Page 8
Skills - Areas of expertise that require training for proficiency. Page 18
Skill Check - A roll made on 3d10 against the skill bonus + 1/2 a statistic made to use a skill. Page 14
Skill Points - Points obtained during character creation that are added into skills as a bonus to that skill. Page 9
Smoke - Rules for the effects of smoke in combat. Page 23
Soldier - A kit focused on combat. Page 8
Statistics - A measure of the qualities of a character. Page 6
Statistic Bonus - A bonus equal to 1/2 the statistic applied to skill rolls. Page 13
Statistic Check - A roll made on 3d10 against a statistic. Page 14
Strength - A statistic that measures the physical strength of

a character. Page 6
Toughness - A statistic that measures how much damage a character can withstand. Page 7
Underwater - Rules for when characters are submerged in fluid. Page 23
Vacuum - The vacuum of space. Extremely harmful. Page 23
Vehicles - Objects that can be piloted with the use of a vehicle key. Page 12

PART 2:
Game Master's Guide

You should only read this section if you are planning on running a game of Alien Outbreak as a game master.

If not, please don't read this book. One of the main concepts of the game is based on the mystery of what the alien is and how it works and reading this book as a player ruins that aspect of the game. If you are still reading this book, you should also read through the Player's Guide before running a game as that book contains the rules that the other players will be following and you should have an idea of what they are capable of.

Your job as GM is to provide the situations that the players will have to deal with. This is broken into two forms: The scenario, and the alien. The scenario is the setting for the characters to act in, the non-player characters (NPCs) and having the setting and NPCs act upon the players and react to their actions. The alien is the main antagonist that the players will be facing. It is a deadly foe that will be hunting them throughout the game. Both can be generated entirely through procedures in this book or designed by hand but it's advised that you at least use the procedural generation as a starting point and tweak the results to your liking. This process will probably take an hour or two, so most of this should be done in advance of the game session.

CHAPTER 5: The Alien

Alien Generation:
This section covers the entirety of creating an alien. It is placed first because most of the mechanics of the alien become apparent during this process as the alien is crafted from the ground up. To speed up the process, it is generally best to roll the statistics, determine how many traits the alien has (1d6+1), roll a % die for each trait the alien will have, roll to see how many weaknesses the alien has if any (1d4-2), roll 1d8 twice to determine it's structure and another 1d8 for it's size, roll to see how many behaviors the alien has if any (1d3-1), rolling to see how the alien reproduces (1d12), then roll to see how many ways the alien cheats if any (1d3-1). Then check to see what each of the results were and apply them. This method gets almost all the rolling out of the way at the start and keeps you from having to flip back and forth through the book repeatedly. If, after rolling up the alien, it seems weak you can instead make there either 1d4 aliens or, if it seems especially weak, 2d6 aliens.

Statistics:
The alien has a number of statistics similar to what the players have, but there are some key differences:
- **Strength** - 1/5 of strength is added to the damage of melee attacks.
- **Toughness** - The amount of damage that the alien can take.
- **Instinct** - When making attacks, noticing details or hiding this is the number that must be rolled against.
- **Speed** - Movement speed is equal to (Speed-5)/2 in 5' squares of movement per action.
- **Special** - How many special points it has, recharges at the start of each act. Special points are used for certain special abilities.

Alien statistics are also rolled in a different manner. Each stat is rolled in order of how they are listed on the page and

is rolled on 3d10. Strength, toughness and instinct also have 5 added to them after the roll.
These statistics may be changed in the generation process.

Traits:
This is the meat of the alien. The alien is essentially defined by these special abilities and they are the main thing that makes the alien dangerous. They get 1d6+1 traits, and roll % die for each to determine what they are. Some traits may require further rolling to determine what variety of that ability the alien has. This is noted as a number in brackets telling you when you have to roll for further details. There are a small amount of abilities which require you to roll for the specifics of a variation. If you roll any duplicates, reroll. The list of traits is below:

1. **Super Strong:** Add 2d10 to the strength score.
2. **Super Tough:** Add 2d10 to the toughness score.
3. **Super Predator:** Add 2d10 to the instinct score.
4. **Sapient:** Has an intelligence score rolled the same way as the rest of the statistics which is used for the alien's reasoning and in place of skills that the players would use intelligence for, starts with the following weapon:

   [1] A wicked melee weapon that deals 1d10+1/5str.

   [2] A gun which may shoot lasers which deals 2d6 and has a range of 60'.

   [3] A razor sharp thrown disc with a range of 20' that deals 1d6 damage but can sticks in the target it.

      [1] Can be triggered to explode for an additional 1d6 damage.

      [2] Can be set as a trap that floats in the air or sticks to a wall and attacks when it detects motion that is not the alien within it's range.

   [4] A shoulder mounted version of the gun the alien can get which makes an attack each round without spending an action.

   [5] A sniper rifle with a range of 200' that deals 1d10 damage.

[6] A net gun with a range of 30' that immobilizes the target until they make a successful agility check to escape).

It has a 40% chance to be wearing body armor, and a 10% chance it has some sort of vehicle. Any attacks with equipment cost 1 special point.

5. **Super Fast:** Add 2d10 to the speed score.
6. **Extra Special:** Add 2d10 to the special score.
7. **Free Ability Use:** One ability that requires the use of special points does not cost any special points to use.
8. **Acid Blood:** When it takes damage it sprays acid blood that hits all adjacent targets, forcing an agility check or they take 1d6 damage, and melts through various things.
9. **Razor Tail:** The alien can make an attack with it's tail that deals 1d8+1/5th strength. On a roll of 10 or less, he impales the target on the tail, requiring a strength check to escape from. It can spend 2 special points to add this effect to a result of 12 or less after the roll has been made.
10. **Squeeze:** The alien can fit through virtually any crack or crevasse.
11. **Natural Armor:** Takes [1d10] less damage per attack taken.
12. **Tentacles:** Can make 2 tentacle attacks as a single action that deals 1d4+1/5th strength damage, each attack can grab on a 5 or less or on a 6 or less at the cost of 2 special points.
13. **Heat Vision:** Can see by heat signature.
14. **X-Ray Vision:** Can see through solid objects by spending 1 special point per minute.
15. **Split:** The alien splits into 2 aliens after it eats or breeds, each of which has 1/2 the amount of special points remaining.
16. **Parasite:** The alien is a parasite. It can crawl into/onto it's host if it grabs some-thing with it's bite attack where it dwells and slowly kills it's host, dealing 1d4 damage per hour. If you try to remove it, it requires a theory check to figure out how the alien is attached, then a biology check at -15skill to remove. It deals 1d8 damage

when removed. This defaults the alien to tiny size.

[1-5] No additional effect.

[6] The alien can spend up to 3 special points to deal an amount of damage equal to the special points spent to it's host and make it roll a morale check or not do an action that the alien doesn't want.

[7] The alien can spend 2 special points to force it's host to make a toughness check or become paralyzed for a minute.

[8] The alien grows as it damages it's host and each hour it is on a person it grows 1 size and it's stats are adjusted. Once it reaches

    [1-3] Small size
    [4-6] Medium size
    [7-8] Large size
    [9] Huge size

it detaches upon which it loses the parasite trait.

[9] The alien reproduces with it's host and after [1d6] hours it implants [1d4-1, min 1] eggs which hatch [1d3] hours later and detaches from the host.

[10] Two effects on this list. (discount "no additional effect" results for this)

17. **Teleportation:** Can spend special points to teleport, it costs 1 special point per 15'.
18. **Climbing:** Can climb at the same rate it can run.
19. **Swimming:** Can swim at the same rate it can run.
20. **Can Live in Space:** The vacuum and cold of space does not harm it.
21. **Cold Blooded:** Does not have a heat signature but needs heat to live.
22. **Dimension Hopping:** Can spend 4 special points to shift in or out of this reality into a different plane. It can pull people and objects through with it. This plane of reality is.

[1] Overlapping with the normal reality (the players take a -10 to perception to see things in this plane, but they can see it. They cannot interact with it, but the alien can pull things into this reality by making an attack that deals no damage).

[2] The reality has a portal leading in and out of it. (the alien cannot warp in or out by spending special points and must use the portal)

[3] The reality overlaps in certain areas (as the first result, but only in certain rooms). The reality is

    [1] A parallel to the normal reality but might be slightly different.

    [2] A completely alien environment. (things get strange)

    [3] A gravity-less void with occasional floating rocks.

    [4] A "reverse reality" from the normal reality. (good is evil, aliens are the "humans" of this world, etc)

23. **No Vitals:** Does not give off any vital signs.
24. **Viral:** The alien is a virus that infects others with an attack against toughness. This can take a few forms:

[1] The infected target starts turning into an alien. (they gain the alien's traits and behaviors over time and begin hunting humans)

[2] The virus is the fetal stage of the alien and it will be birthed from the infected person eventually.

[3] The virus functions as Poison.

[4] The virus is an alternate form that the alien can turn into.

    The virus is spread in one of the following ways:

    [1] Airborne.
    [2] Waterborne.
    [3] Bloodborne/Fluidborne.
    [4] Foodborne.
    [5] Contact.
    [6] Weird. (such as eye contact, talking about it, etc)

25. **Second Alien Type:** Roll up a second type of alien which has 1 less trait than it rolls.

    [1] The aliens are ambivalent to each other.
    [2] The alien with higher instinct hunts the other type.
    [3] The aliens hate each other.
    [4] The aliens are working together.

26. **Drink Blood:** When the alien bites it grabs on a 15 or lower. If it grabs it deals 1d4 damage to the target each round.
27. **Evolving:** Gains a new trait every time it shows up.
28. **Hyper Adapting:** Gains a new trait every time it takes damage.
29. **Camouflage:** Can cut the results of it's stealth checks in half by spending 3 special points.
30. **Invisibility:** Cannot be directly detected visibly.
    [1] Constant.
    [2-4] Must spend 1 special point per round.
    [5] Must spend 2 special points per round.
    [6] Must spend 1 special point per minute.
31. **Psychic Powers:** Has psychic abilities that it can spend special points to use. Roll 1d4-1(minimum 1) to see how many psychic powers it has.
    [1] Mental Communication. (costs 1 special point per message)
    [2] Mind Thrust. (instinct based attack, range 30', 1d8+1/5th instinct damage to morale, costs 2 special points)
    [3] Mind Control. (instinct vs intelligence attack, costs 5 special points per attack and per minute)
    [4] Telekinesis. (make an attack with a range of 20' by throwing an object w/i 30' at a target, costs 2 special points)
    [5] Track by Thought. (can detect thoughts of things within 60' by spending 2 special points)
32. **Echolocation:** Can detect through sound alone.
33. **Poison:** One of it's attacks has a poison on it, when it hits and deals damage the poison takes effect after the encounter ends. The poison lasts until cured with a medicine check. There are a variety of poison types:
    [1] Deals 1d6 damage.
    [2] Reduces strength by 1d4.
    [3] Reduces perception by 1d4.
    [4] Reduces intelligence by 1d4.
    [5] Reduces agility by 1d4.
    [6] Paralysis (can take no actions) for 1d6 rounds.
    [7] Hallucinations for 1d6min.

[8] Paranoia for 1d6 hours.
[9] Violent rage for 1d6 rounds.
[10] Pregnant by 1d2-1(minimum 1) aliens.
The poison has an onset time of:
[1] Instant.
[2] [1d3] rounds.
[3] [1d4] rounds.
[4] [1d6] rounds.
[5] [1d6] minutes.
[6] [1d3] hours.
It takes effect every:
[1] Round.
[2] 2 rounds.
[3] [1d6] rounds.
[4] Minute.
[5] [1d3] minutes.
[6] [1d6] minutes.
[7] Hour.
[8] [1d3] hours.

34. **Webs:** Can spin webs which reduce the speed of those within by 1/2, and can spend 1 special point to spit a web as an attack with a range of 20'.
35. **Hypnotic Chittering:** Can spend 3 special points to start chittering, all that can hear it lose 1d4 morale per round. It does not take an action to maintain, but it costs 1 special point per round to maintain.
36. **Flight:** Can fly at the same rate it can move across the ground.
37. **Minions:** Has weaker aliens that help it, there are 3d3 of them and they have 15 on each stat and 1 trait. roll a d4, on a 4 the trait varies from minion to minion. They treat the main alien as more important than itself. They have a bite/generic melee attack that deals 1d4+1/5 strength.
38. **Regeneration:** Heals [1d4] damage at the start of each round.
39. **Burrowing:** Can move through soft ground freely.
40. **Swarm:** The alien is a swarm. It can fly, and move

through all terrain freely. Furthermore, they cannot be hurt by single target attacks.

41. **Claws:** Can make 2 claw attacks as a single action that deal 1d6+1/5th strength.
42. **Lurching:** Reduce movement speed by 1/2, but whenever it moves roll 1d6 and move an additional amount of 5' increments equal to the roll.
43. **Blood Rage:** When below 1/2 hp the alien only rolls 1d20 for attacks and deals +3 more damage.
44. **Dust:** The alien can spend a special point to spew out a 20' cloud of dust which has an effect which is determined when the alien is rolled up:
    [1] As the poison trait.
    [2] Any people within must roll a perception check or fall unconscious for 1d6min.
    [3] Players within must roll an extra die for non-damage rolls.
    [4] Players within deal 1/2 damage.
45. **Super Hearing:** Can hear heartbeats and pretty much every-thing else.
46. **Dark-Vision:** Can see in the dark.
47. **Fluid Body:** The alien is a liquid. This cuts the speed in half, cuts any damage taken in half. Furthermore, the size determines how much space it can cover when fully spread out; tiny covers 5sq', small covers 10sq', medium covers 20sq', large covers 45sq', huge covers 80sq'. The alien can only attack creatures on it's space unless it has a special attack that specifies otherwise. It can also use this ability to move through extremely small spaces.
48. **Acid Spit:** The alien has a special spit attack with a range of 20' that deals 1d6 damage to the target and continues to do so for 1d3 rounds. Costs 1 special point.
49. **Spines:** The alien is covered in spines. When a melee attack is made against the alien, the attacker must roll agility or take 1d4 damage. The alien's melee attacks deal an extra 2 damage. roll a d4, on a 4 the alien can shoot the spines with a range of 15' at the cost of 2 special points, this is 2 attacks that each deal 1d4 damage.

50. Cybernetics: The alien has robotic parts built into it.

   [1] Laser eyes. (40' range, 1d10 damage, costs 1 special point)

   [2] Robotic limbs. (+10str, +5 speed)

   [3] Robotic Armor. (+20 toughness)

   [4] Drones. (has 2d3 drones which it can move around as the "minions" trait)

   [5] Built in gun with a range of 60' dealing 1d10 damage and costs 1 special point to fire.

   [6] Roll twice more on this roll.

51. Shapeshifting: The alien can shape shift for 3 special points. NPCs can turn out to be the alien, the players might also turn out the be the alien for a scene if they split up. Periodically pass notes to the players that tell them various red herrings, are blank, or tell them that this scene has them as the alien and that they are somewhere else and to act as they feel the alien would. They are also told not to discuss the notes.

52. Plant Cells: When the alien takes more than 5 damage from a single attack, part of it's body is severed. Even a single cell of the alien can grow into a full alien. The body parts start at 5hp and grow 1 hp per minute. As they gain hp they grow in size until they are the full alien. Partly grown aliens can act, but are pathetic enough where they don't need to be fully stated out but still have the traits of the alien.

53. Shed Skin: The alien can shed it's skin at the cost of 2 special points and 2 damage. This removes any foreign effects from the alien and, if the alien has eaten at least 1 creature within the past few hours, it can spend an additional 5 special points to increase by one size.

54. Traps: Can set traps for 2 special points which need a perception check to be noticed.

   [1] A net or glue trap which requires an agility check to escape.

   [2] A spike trap which either people can fall into or that swings at them dealing 1d8 damage.

   [3] A spur trap/caltrops which deals 1d4 damage and

halves the movement speed until a surgery check is made to remove them.

    [4] A gas trap which forces a toughness check or the target passes out for 1d4 minutes.

    [5] A tempting item laid out for an ambush.

    [6] A portal trap which warps them to a cage that the alien has set up some-where. Traps may be organic or technological in nature, depending on the nature of the alien.

55.   **Aura:** The alien has an aura of:

    [1] Fear which deals 1 morale damage per round.

    [2] Stench which distracts those within it and gives them a penalty of [1d4] to the result of rolls they make.

    [3] Cold that deals 1 damage per round.

    [4] Static electricity that deals 1 damage per 5' moved through.

    The aura goes out [1d6*5]!

56.   **Slime:** The alien leaves slime everywhere it goes it is.

    [1] Sticky and requires an agility check to move through without getting stuck on it until you make an agility check to get out.

    [2] Slippery which requires an agility check when passing through or they fall down.

    [3] Acidic and dealing 1d4 damage to those passing through it and may burn through the floor.

57.   **Corrupting Influence:** Interacting with the alien causes the alien's influence to spread.

    [1] This requires a successful critical attack.

    [2] This requires a successful attack.

    [3] This requires contact with the alien.

    [4] Anyone who hears the alien's vocalizations is affected.

    [5] Anyone who sees the alien's eyes is affected.

    Any method of the affecting a non-alien allows the affected creature a morale check to resist. After affected, the creature starts to show symptoms after

    [1] 1d4 hours.

    [2] 2d6 hours.

    [3] 1d4 days.

[4] 2d6 days.
The symptoms, once they manifest, are:
[1] Losing 2d4 morale and the alien can spend [1d4] special points to force a morale check in the victim to take control of them for 1 round.
[2] Losing 1d4 morale and the victim must make a morale check to take an action that goes against the alien.
[3] Loses 1d6 morale, the victim gains the corrupting influence and one of the alien's abilities and the victim manifests another set of symptoms rolled on a d2 rather than a d4 after 1d4 hours.
[4] Roll on this list twice.
58. **Long Attack:** One of the alien's attacks can hit from anv additional 5' away.
59. **Voice Imitation:** The alien can imitate sounds and voices that it has heard.
60. **Tremor-sense:** Can "see" vibrations in surfaces it is touching.
61. **Opposable Thumbs:** Can manipulate objects as well as a human can. Does not require arms or even limbs.
62. **Abomination:** Double the amount of limbs the alien has, the alien has an extra action per round which must be used for an attack.
63. **Death Throes:** When the alien dies it continues to act for [1d4] rounds, it cannot move during these rounds and must use all it's actions to attack. While in it's death throes it has infinite special points.
64. **Symbiotes:** The alien has tiny symbiotes living in it. When it makes it's bite attack or takes damage from a melee attack the target has to roll an agility check or some symbiotes are transferred to the target. These symbiotes effect humans differently from how they affect the alien.
[1] They sap nutrients and decrease their hosts strength by 1/minute.
[2] They propagate throughout their host and 1d4 hours later the host must roll a toughness check (if they make the check it resets the countdown on the check) or

vomit the symbiotes up which deals 1d6 damage.

[3] They mutate the host after 1d4 hours who gains a trait that the alien has but deals 1d6 damage when it occurs.

[4] The alien can detect and track the symbiotes and effectively knows where any hosts are at all times.

[5] The symbiotes affect the mind of their host and deal 1 morale damage per minute as the host goes mad.

65. **Second Form:** If killed, the alien swells in size by 1, gains 1d3 traits.
66. **Gory Kills:** When the alien kills some-thing it mutilates it horribly and all that see the act must make a morale check or take 1d6 morale damage.
67. **Robotic:** The alien is non-biological. Checks involving knowledge of the alien are made as mechanical checks rather than biology checks. The alien can repair itself by taking pieces of mechanical equipment and grafting them onto their body. This takes 2d6 minutes and heals 2d6 hp. It can also refill its special pool in the same way.
68. **Mineral:** The alien has a mineral structure rather than an animal structure. It is immune to chemical compounds that affect living creatures (poison, medicine, etc), does not count as alive, and gets +10 toughness.
69. **Scary:** Increase all morale damage dealt by the alien by [1d3].
70. **Trophies:** The alien takes trophies from it's kills and:
    [1] Wears them.
    [2] Displays them at it's nest. (Or around, if there is no nest)
    [3] Tosses them at people from the shadows to scare them. The first time the trophies they deal 1d4 morale damage unless the target makes a morale check.
71. **Scabs:** When damaged the alien develops 1 scab per time injured 1d4 minutes later. These scabs have [1d4] toughness and take damage first as body armor. Scabs that take damage do not develop scabs. Roll 1d8, on an 8 scabs can develop scabs if they are damaged.
72. **Sixth Sense:** The alien cannot be ambushed and, on the first round of combat, gets 1.5 times the number of

actions it would normally get.

73. **Strange Time:** The alien interacts strangely with time.

[1] It can move 4th dimensionally by spending [1d3] special points. (It vanishes and appears [1d6] rounds later. It can take actions while out of time)

[2] As one but it can move other things (such as people it is grabbing) with it.

[3] It experiences time backwards. (when first found, the alien is dead with a bunch of wounds all over it. The alien can only be killed in the room it is found. When the alien is damaged, it's wounds disappear and it moves in a backwards "rewound" fashion)

[4] The alien can "undo" events affecting it for [1d6] special points. (This is mainly attacks against it but could be things such as trackers being put on it and the like as well. It does not include things that do not directly physically affect it such as the players gaining information on it or seeing it)

[5] Roll twice more on this roll.

74. **Super-Sonic Scream:** The alien can spend 2 special points to make a scream attack which:

[1] Deals 1d6 damage to all within 30'.

[2] Pushes any-one closer than 30' to the alien to 30' away.

[3] Is terrifying and deals 1d6 morale damage.

[4] Stuns any within 30' unless they make a toughness check for [1d3] rounds.

[5] Pulls 1 target within 30' adjacent to the alien.

[6] Roll twice more on this list.

75. **Scent Sense:** The alien can locate other creatures within [2d4]*5' by scent.

76. **Trap Square:** The alien can spend 1 special point to mark a 5' square adjacent to them. This space moves with them. If some-one enters this square, the alien can make an attack against them immediately with an attack/weapon rolled at the creation of the alien. If the square is made with an attack that can hit non-adjacent to them, it does not have to be adjacent to the alien, and can be

within the reach/range of that attack instead. The space remains marked for [1d6] rounds.

77. **Trample:** The alien can move it's speed and make an attack that deals 1d6+1/5strength damage and knocks the target over.
78. **Stretch Limits:** The alien can spend 1 special point to deal 1d4 damage to itself to:
    [1] Reroll a roll it just made, such as an attack roll, damage roll, or other attribute roll.
    [2] Extend the reach of one of it's attacks by 5'.
    [3] Increase it's movement speed by 10' for 1 round.
79. **Tongue:** The alien has a long tongue 10' long.
    [1] It is razor sharp and can be used as an attack dealing 1d6+1/5str.
    [2] Is sticky and can be used as an attack that pulls you 10' towards the alien if it hits.
    [3] It can use as a hand with an opposable thumb.
    [4] Two effects on this list.
80. **Unpredictable Movement:** If any attacks miss the alien it moves 5' in a direction of it's choice and regains a special point.
81. **Charge:** If the alien moves before making an attack, they add +1 to the damage per 10' moved. If the alien only has one action it can move up to 1/2 it's speed and make an attack as a single action.
82. **Leap:** The alien can jump as high and far as it can move in a turn without having to roll.
83. **Improved Attack:** The damage of one of the alien's attacks is increased by 1 step.
84. **Static Buildup:** As the alien moves, it accrues static electricity which it can discharge:
    [1] As a melee attack dealing 1dX where X is the number of actions spent to move.
    [2] As a ranged attack dealing 1d4 with a range of 10' per number of actions spent to move.
85. **Fluid Sacs:** When damage is dealt to the alien, the alien can make spend 2 special points to have the attack hit a fluid filled sac on the alien, bursting it and spewing:

[1] Poison as the trait.
[2] Acid that deals 1d6 damage.
[3] A sticky goo which immobilizes those within it until they make an agility check to escape.
[4] A quick drying plaster-like subject that dries in 1d4 rounds and requires a strength check to break out of (but it can be broken by others making attacks against it and has 10hp). The sac bursting is an attack which targets all within 15' of it.

86. **Plasma Body:** The alien is composed of plasma, damage it deals cannot be healed since it disintegrates whatever it touches and it only takes 1/2 damage since it is not a cohesive mass.
87. **Drone Body:** The alien is a featureless blob incapable of defending itself, but controls a more dangerous body remotely. The remote body is what is rolled up for alien creation, while the blob has 0 strength, 10 toughness, instinct equal to the remote body, 7 speed, 0 special and is tiny sized. If the helpless body is killed the remote body is as well, but not the other way around. The remote body is expendable and can be "repaired" by the helpless body at a rate of 1d8 toughness per 10 minutes.
88. **Sneak Attack:** When the alien ambushes the players and hits one of them with an attack, the player must roll a perception check or take an additional [1d3] damage.
89. **Wide Strikes:** When the alien misses an attack by 5 or less, it still deals 1/5 strength damage to the target.
90. **Secondary Strike:** One of the attacks that the alien can make has an additional attack as the same action as making that one. (Example: If apppplied for bite it would be able to bite twice as a single action, if applied to claws it would be able make 3 claw attacks as a single action)
91. **Disease:** Coming in contact with the alien or being near it for prolonged periods of time causes the target to have to make a toughness check or contract a disease. This can be cured with a medicine check once the disease has been studied using theoretical science.
[1] The disease makes the victim into a hungry mess

who loses their ability to think rationally and they must make morale checks or eat whatever meat is around (including living creatures) if they make the check they take 1d3 morale damage.

    [2] Victims of the disease take -5 perception to notice the alien.

    [3] Victims of the disease decrease one of their stats by 1d4 per hour.

        [1] Strength.
        [2] Toughness.
        [3] Perception.
        [4] Intelligence.
        [5] Agility.
        [6] Morale.

92. **Horn:** The alien has horns or antlers of some sort which it can use to make an attack that deals 1d8+1/5strength. The alien can move 10' before this attack or 5' after instead of 5' before or after.
93. **Hunting Companion:** The alien has a subordinate companion alien which is rolled up as a separate alien that rolls 2d10+5 for it's stats except for instinct which is rolled as 3d10+5, cannot have an intelligence score or use weapons and deals 1 die step lower for damage. An alien with this trait gets -5 instinct.
94. **Swallow Whole:** The alien can eat any-one it grabs with it's mouth as an action by making another attack roll against the grabbed person. If it succeeds, the grabbed person is eaten; they remain alive but take 1d4 damage each round and the only action they can take is to make a strength check to escape.
95. **Blades:** The alien has [1d2] long razor sharp blades somewhere on it's body which it can attack with as a single action. It can be either organic bone blades or metal blades implanted on it. It can make a number of attacks equal to the number of blades it has. Each blade deals 1d6 damage and on a roll of 10 or less cause the target to take 1 damage per round until they are cured by a surgery check which takes 1 round. Roll 1d4, on a 4 the alien can

spend 3 special points to grow another blade that lasts for 1 minute.

96. Roar: The alien can spend 1 special point to let out a blood chilling roar that deals 1d6 morale damage if people within 30' of it fail a morale check.

97. Beak: The alien has a beak, instead of grabbing with it's basic attack on a roll of 10 or less it bites out a chunk of them, and the damage dealt with that attack cannot be healed.

98. Accrue: The alien can spend 1 special point to absorb:
[1] Organic matter.
[2] Mechanical parts.
into itself, increasing it's toughness by 1d4. If the matter or parts can resist, they get a toughness roll to do so. For every [2d3] things it absorbs it grows in size by 1. (It does not gain any additional toughness for the size increases however)

99. Fast Learning: If the alien sees some-thing done, they learn how to do it immediately.

100. Oily Secretions: The alien secretes an oil:
[1] Constantly.
[2] By spending 1 special point. (it takes an action to start secreting, but does not take an action to maintain secreting it. It costs 1 special point per round it is active)
The oil is:
   [1] Slippery and requires an agility check to move through without falling over.
   [2] Flammable.
   [3] Acidic and deals 1d4 damage to those passing through it.
The oil spreads 5' around the alien per use/per round.

If you roll duplicates of the same trait apply that trait twice if possible, or reroll if it wouldn't make any sense.

Weakness:

Weaknesses are the flip-side of traits. These are abilities that limit the power of the alien and are designed to add some flavor to how the player can fight the alien should they figure out it's weakness. Roll 1d4-2 to see how many weaknesses the alien has. If the result is 0 or negative, the alien has no weaknesses.

1. **Limited Vision:** Can only see:
   [1] Moving targets.
   [2] Infrared.
   [3] Red to green.
   [4] Light blindness. (cannot see in bright light)
   [4] Green to violet.
   [5] Ultraviolet.
   [6] Sound.
2. **Blind:** Cannot see at all and must rely on hearing or other senses.
3. **Deaf:** Cannot hear.
4. **No Mouth:** Cannot grab with it's default attack.
5. **Fear:** Is afraid of:
   [1] Fire.
   [2] Light.
   [3] Darkness.
   [4] Small rodents.
   [5] Specific sounds. (such as bells)
   [6] Things bigger than it.
6. **Weak to Fire or Cold:** Takes double damage from:
   [1] Fire.
   [2] Cold.
7. **Low Damage:** The aliens attacks deal 1 die step less. (1d8 to 1d6, 1d6 to 1d4, 1d4 to 1d3, 1d3 to 1)
8. **Odd Appetite:** Needs to consume some kind of odd material as food.
   [1-3] Steel/metal.
   [4-5] Radioactive material.
   [6] Space. (actually consumes volume/area)
9. **Stationary:** The alien cannot move and instead grows into the area. Double it's toughness and the reach of it's

attacks. It grows at a rate of 1d4*10sq' every 2d20 minutes.
10. **Slow Reactions:** The alien goes at the end of the turn instead of at the start.
11. **Charge Up:** The alien starts with 0 special points, but can have an amount of points equal to the amount rolled for the special stat. It must:
   [1] Spend an action in combat to gain [1d4] special points which last for 1 minute.
   [2] Eat a living creature to gain 1d8 special points.
   [3] It gains [1d6] special points per hour.
   [4] It gains 2 special points which last for 1 minute whenever it takes damage.
12. **Staggerable:** The alien takes penalties on rolls from damage in the same way that a human would.
13. **Low Statistic:** Reduce:
   [1] Strength by half.
   [2] Toughness by half.
   [3] Instinct by half.
   [4] Speed by half.
   [5] Special by half.
   [6] Roll twice and half both stats.
14. **Aquatic:** For every minute outside of water, the alien takes 1 damage.
15. **Sunlight Sensitivity:** The alien is sensative to sunlight and:
   [1] Takes 1 damage per round in direct sunlight.
   [2] Has 1/2 instinct for making attack rolls and perception checks while in direct sunlight.
16. **Loud:** The alien either emits some sort of noise, moves loudly or otherwise announces it's presence before it actually shows up.
17. **Unhealing:** Any loss to the alien's toughness is permanent.
18. **Stupid:** The alien is more likely to fall for traps or do what the players are expecting it to do.
19. **Limited Special:** Special does not refill at the start of each act..

20. **Roll Twice:** take both results, and reroll any conflicting results.

Structure:
These rolls determine the body type of the alien. Roll on this chart twice and reroll the second result if it conflicts with the first until the two make sense.
1. **No Legs:** Has no legs and takes -4 speed, but gets +6 toughness.
2. **No Arms:** Has no arms and gains +2 speed.
3. **Biped:** Has 2 legs, +1 speed.
4. **Quadruped:** Has 4 legs, +2 speed.
5. **More than Four Legs:** Roll 4d4 for the number of legs, for every 2 legs above 2 it gets +2 speed.
6. **Arms:** The alien has arms and can hold things. Each arm grants +1 str.
    - **[1-5]** 1d2 arms.
    - **[5-6]** 1d3 arms.
    - **[7-8]** 1d4 arms.
    - **[9-10]** 1d6 arms.
7. **Head:** has a head separate from it's body and gains +2 instinct.
8. Roll twice more.

Size:
This is a measure of how large the alien is. This can greatly affect the statistics of the alien as well as how far away it can attack characters with melee attacks
1. **Tiny:** About the size of a house cat, 1'-3'. +20 speed, -10 strength and toughness.
2. **Small:** About the size of a medium sized dog, 3'-5'. +10 speed, -5 strength and toughness.
3-5. **Medium:** About the size of a human being, 5-8'. No modifiers.
6-7. **Large:** About the size of a mid-sized car, 9'-15'-5 speed, +10 strength and toughness. Can make melee attacks from 10' away.
8. **Huge:** About the size of an elephant or larger, 16'-25'.

-10 speed, +15 strength and toughness. Can make melee attacks from 10' away.

Behavior:

While you ultimately control the alien, behaviors are a guideline to add some kind of personality to the alien. Roll 1d3-1 to see how many behaviors the alien has. If the result is 0 or negative, the alien has no special behaviors.

1. **Nesting:** The alien creates a hidden nest where it will generally hang around.
2. **Queen and Drones:** There is one queen who births a large brood of 4d6 aliens every once in a while. The queen is automatically Huge and has 1/2 speed of her brood.
3. **Solitary:** The alien will only hunt individual targets.
4. **Pack:** There are 2d4 aliens and they hunt as a group.
5. **Run Away:** The alien is a coward and will not directly confront the players.
6. **Rampage:** Once the alien starts fighting, it does not stop.
7. **Hit and Run:** The alien uses hit and run tactics.
8. **Play with your Food:** The alien will torture their prey and some-times let them go to hunt them later.
9. **Grudge:** The alien will go after whoever hurts it first with an infinite vengeance.
10. **Sapient Intelligence:** The alien is as smart or smarter than humans and is from a species that has technology and can understand tech after spending a few minutes with it. It is smart, will set traps, and values it's own life. They may or may not be armed and have equipment.
11. **Cyclical:** The alien only needs to eat [1d4] things before it goes back into a hibernation state for many years.
12. **Cautious:** The alien will observe the players while hidden to learn what they can do before engaging them directly. It also retreats more.
13. **Searching:** The alien is searching for a particular object or artifact which is up to you to decide what it is and why the alien is after it. Once it finds and obtains this

object it will try to escape with it.
14. **Capture:** The alien will attempt to single out and capture other creatures and bring them to an isolated spot to eat in piece.
15. **Wear Down:** The alien is more than content to outlast the players rather than risk itself in direct confrontations.
16. **Ambush:** The alien will more often ambush the players and be smarter about it.
17. **Defensive:** The alien is mainly reactive, but after being attacked may become more aggressive later on in the game.
18. **Protective:** The alien is actually protecting a certain NPC. This really only works if the players have a reason to be hostile towards an NPC.
19. **Scavenger:** The alien is primarily a scavenger and is content to eat corpses. Make sure to write in some accidents to kill off some NPCs to showcase this.
20. **Conditional Trait Usage:** Select one of the alien's traits. The alien only uses this trait under situations of duress such as if it has been damaged in combat.

Reproduction:

This section is semi-optional. If you don't want to deal with this kind of material either because it makes you uncomfortable or because it isn't appropriate for the player group there is nothing wrong with ignoring this section in it's entirety. The point of having details for how the alien reproduces is both to add challenge since it can easily lead to the players fighting a large number of aliens, as well as adding a sense that this is a real creature that lives and breathes.

1-2. **Asexual Reproduction:** Can reproduce without other aliens.
3. **Reproduction Attack:** Can reproduce with a special ovipositor attack that deals 1d6 damage and costs 2 special points. The reproduction ends with the birth of:
    [1] 1 egg.
    [2] 1 live birth.

[3] 1d3-1 (minimum 1) live births.
[4] a brood of 4d4 eggs.

After getting impregnated, the player must make a morale check or feel the need to protect the eggs because they are their children; NPCs automatically fail this check.

4. **Multistage Life-Form:** The alien has 3 stages of life. A newborn is 2 sizes smaller and only has 1 of the traits of the alien. An adolescent has all the traits but one and is 1 size smaller. The adult is the alien as normal. It takes [1d4] hours to mature to the next stage after birth and the adult is the only form in which it can reproduce, which it does as per sexual reproduction.

5. **Symbiotic Reproduction:** A second alien type is required to properly reproduce. This is identical to sexual reproduction, but requires it to mate with a specific alien. If there is no second alien type present, roll one up. It defaults to this method of reproduction.

6-9. **Sexual Reproduction:** Multiple aliens are required to reproduce.
[1-4] 2 aliens.
[5] 2d3 aliens.
[6] 2d4+1 aliens.
This process takes 1d4 hours and yields:
[1-5] 1 alien.
[6-10] 1d4 aliens.
[11-14] 1d6 aliens.
[15-17] 2d8 aliens.
[18-19] 4d8 aliens.
[20] 3d20 aliens.
The aliens cannot reproduce for another:
[1] 2d10 hours.
[2] 1d4 days.
[3] 1d8 days.
[4] 2d8 days.
The aliens born are:
[1-3] Eggs that hatch after 2d4 hours.
[4] Live birth.

10-12. **Does not Reproduce:** The alien cannot reproduce.

Cheating:

The alien does not function on the same ruleset as the players, so cheating is not entirely accurate as a name. These are abilities that change the core mechanics of how the alien works in a way that can easy be likened to cheating were the players to figure out how this section works. Roll 1d4-2 to see how many cheating abilities the alien has. If the result is 0 or negative, the alien has no cheating abilities.

1. **Plot Convenient Location:** Can appear or go pretty much anywhere even if it wouldn't make any sense. Use sparingly.
2. **Cheat Death:** If there is only one alien, or one alien left, it does not die and continues to plague the players at inconvenient moments. Alternatively, this is the "there was another one" trope, where you kill the alien only to surprise them with a second one later on.
3. **Weird Dice:** Whenever the alien rolls a die or dice, roll a die or dice of your choosing. This can change throughout the game.
4. **Act out of Turn:** Once per combat, the alien can interrupt a player's turn to take it's own turn instead. The original player's turn resumes after the alien finishes it's turn.
5. **Abstract Health:** Damage that the alien takes is described but not tracked, it only is killed when you says it is.
6. **Fake out Jump Scare:** Freely set up situations where the players think the alien is hiding some-where, but it's not. Feel free to have it ambush them and get a free turn in.
7. **Meta Knowledge:** Assume that the alien knows all of the actions of the players, even if the alien has no way of knowing that information.
8. **Tragic Act 3:** When determining the dynamic difficulty score, the number is always negative and the GM just picks it.
9. **Bullshit Superpower:** Midway through the game you select a new trait that the alien spontaneously gains.

10. **Infinite Special:** Do not track the spending of special points.
11. **Wound Points:** Instead of taking damage the alien gets wounds. If it is hit by an attack that would deal 4 or more damage it gets a wound, it can sustain a number of wounds equal to 1/4 its toughness. If hit by an attack that would deal less than 4 damage it is a "glancing blow" that has no effect.
12. **Landmark Movement:** Instead of having a direct movement speed the alien moves from "landmark" to "landmark." It can move to a number of landmarks equal to 1/4 speed. Landmarks can be things like a table in a room or a person.
13. **Staggered Turn:** If the alien has multiple actions it goes for each action beyond the first.
14. **Special Checks:** Instead of spending special points, abilities that would cost special points require a special check. This check has a penalty equal to what would be the cost-1.
15. **Condensed Statistics Block:** The alien's toughness and strength are combined into an attribute called Body. Body is equal to the higher of strength or toughness. Speed and instinct are similarly combined into a stat called Cunning.
16. **Skills:** The alien has a number of skill points equal to twice its instinct score+10. It's skills are: attack, stealth, secondary movement(climb, fly, etc), sense motive. The skill points are distributed by a priority system. Roll a d10 for each skill that the alien could end up using; the highest roll gets 1/2 the skill points, the second highest gets 1/2 the remaining, the third highest gets 1/2 the remaining and so forth.
17. **Focused Targeting:** The alien "picks on" a particular player determined randomly and will target them more than 1/2 the time.
18. **Recharge Abilities:** Instead of spending special points to use abilities, the aliens abilities are on a timer of their special point cost number of rounds after each use

before they can be used again. The alien loses the "special" ability score.
19. **Skin Suit:** One of the NPCS is actually the alien in disguise as a human. It doesn't really matter if this makes sense or not since it should be a surprise sometime in Act 2 or 3.
20. **Secret Notes:** Pass out notes to the players at various times throughout the game. The content of these notes can be details that only they see or just dummy notes to make people nervous. Feel free to use this to turn players against each other by lying about details as well.

The Description:
After you've finished generating the alien, it is important to go over and figure exactly what has been created. Look through it's abilities and statistics and come up with what this thing looks and acts like. What it looks like is very important and should include details that tell a bit about the alien's abilities. For example, if an alien has the slime trait it should mention that it is oozing slime in the description. Obviously, not all abilities have a visible component. When the players first encounter the alien it is a good idea to read some part of this description to them so that they have a good idea of what they are looking at. Because of this, it is also a good idea to write the description as if it were for the first encounter with the alien, rather than just a clinical list of features. A name is not needed for your alien since it is an unknown creature and the players will likely come up with a name for it in the course of the game. There are a number of sample aliens listed in the back of this book for examples and quick play.

Running the Alien:
Think of the alien as being "your" character in the game. That being said, you shouldn't try to "win," but rather act out what the alien would do in the situation applying as much logic as you can. As a GM, you should strive to facilitate the

game to create a fun experience for yourself and the other players. The alien follows the same general guidelines and play of the characters, but you shouldn't tell the players what the alien is doing unless they can see it's actions. Keep the alien hidden as much as you can while keeping it a constant threat. When the alien does appear, describe what it is doing in detail and make sure that it is strange and frightening. The alien should not be passive either. While the players are doing their thing, the alien should be as well. If all the players are working on hour long projects, have the alien drop in on one of them and attack. If the players are hunting it down, have it clinging to the ceiling and drop down on them. If the players need a particular NPC to fix their ship and get out of there they had better be watching over that NPC; and if they do manage to fix their ship, guess what's hiding in the cargo hold. The players should need to be on their toes in order to survive.

Alien Rules:

Outside of combat, the alien generally follows the same rules as the player. In combat is a different story; while many of the actions they can take have equivalent player actions, the combat rules for the alien are different enough where they are discussed here in their entirety. It is important to not tell the players any of the rules for the alien.

Each round, the alien goes first unless it has an ability that says otherwise or it is ambushed by the players. In the case of the later, it goes second. Conversely, if the alien is the one doing the ambushing it gets 2 turns on the first round.

The number of actions that the alien gets on each of it's turns is determined by the number of players in the game aside from you. The alien gets 1 action, plus an additional action if there are more than 3 players, and a further action for every 2 players more than 3. For example, in a game with 4 players the alien would have 2 actions, with 5 players it would have 3, and with 9 it would have 5. If there is more than one alien in the game (either multiple of the same type or different species) the amount of

actions the alien gets is reduced by 1 to a minimum of 1. The actions that the alien can take in combat are:
- Move up to it's movement speed.
- Make an attack with one of the attacks generated for the alien.
- Make a basic attack.
- Interact with an object. (As per the player rules for this, but keep in mind that not all aliens have arms)
- Attempt to hide. (The players cannot have line of sight for the alien to be able to take this action)
- Common sense action. (This is essentially a catch-all for actions that might come up)

Since the alien does not have skills, whatever rolls it has to make are statistic checks. Don't bother rolling any checks for the alien outside of combat and especially not when the players are not observing it; assume it succeeds.

The alien's basic attack is a melee attack that is representative of a generic bite or bodyslam or the like. It deals 1d8 damage + 1/5 strength and a roll of 10 or less allows the alien to grab the target. Grabbing a target is not an action and can only be done immediately after the attack that allows for it. While the alien has someone grabbed it moves at 1/2 speed with the grabbed target and it cannot use it's basic attack, but any attacks it makes automatically hit and the grabbed target cannot move. The alien can end a grab any time without using an action, but if the grabbed target wishes to escape they must make a strength check as an action.

If the alien takes damage it's toughness is reduced by the damage taken. If this damage reduces the alien's toughness to 0 or less it is killed. Unlike humans, the alien takes no penalties on rolls of any sort due to damage.

CHAPTER 6: The Scenario

Now that you have created your alien, it is time to move on to the scenario. The scenario is considerably more complex than the alien and going by method of pure generation takes much longer. While there are rules presented here for pure generation it is recommended that the scenario be designed to make the alien more interesting. For example, if the alien is good at climbing it might be interesting to make the setting have at least one large vertical shaft. Similarily, if the alien is aquatic or good at swimming put a body of water in the setting to show this off. The benefit of generation on the other hand, provides a lot more specifics for the setting such as what items armory has or adds small details such as supply closet or the like.

Generating the Setting:

First the category of which type of setting is determined by rolling 1d4.
1. **Space Ship**
2. **Otherworld Colony**
3. **Asteroid Mining Facility**
4. **Isolated Nature** (probably not on Earth)

These setting types are not the end all-be all, but more a set of starting points and common tropes of the genre.

Each setting type has consistencies both within themselves and compared to the others, but use their own charts to determine their specifics such as the layout, features and reason that the players are there.

After determining the type of setting, the features are rolled for. Each setting type has some rooms that will always be present, a number of rooms and generally how many NPCs will be there. Any restrictions on layout also listed here.

Space Ship:

Will always have the following rooms:
- **Cockpit**
- **Engine Room**

- **Cryo Bay**
- **Airlock**

Possible Rooms:
1. **Hanger**
2. **Common Room**
3. **Armory**
4. **Bathroom**
5-6. **Vents**
6. **Med Bay**
7. **Cargo Bay**
8. **Kitchen**
9. **Supply Closet**
10-12. **Escape Pods**

Number of Rooms: 2d4+4+Hallways
NPCs: 1d6-1

Otherworld Colony:
Will always have the following rooms:
- **Common Room**
- **Furnace Room**
- **Sewers**

Possible Rooms:
1-4. **Bedroom**
5-6. **Office**
7. **Courtyard**
8. **Med Bay**
9. **Cargo Bay**
10. **Kitchen**
11. **Freezer**
12. **Science Lab**
13. **Holding Cells**
14. **Armory**
15. **Security Room**
16. **Hanger**
17. **Barracks**
18-19. **Vents**
20-22. **Supply Closet**
23. **Trash Disposal**

24-25.   Bathroom
Layout: Broken into 2 wings. Both wings must have sewers
Rooms in Each Wing: 2d4+2+hallways rooms
NPCS: 20d10

Asteroid Mining Facility:
Will always have the following rooms:
- **Mine Shaft**
- **Common Room**
- **Office**
- **Furnace Room**
- **Hanger**

Possible Rooms:
- **1-2.** Sewers
- **3.** Courtyard
- **4-7.** Bedroom
- **8-9.** Bathroom
- **10.** Cargo Bay
- **11.** Med Bay
- **12.** Kitchen
- **13.** Freezer
- **14.** Armory
- **15-16.** Security Lab
- **17.** Vents
- **18-19.** Supply Closet
- **20.** Trash Disposal

Layout: Broken into 2 wings. Both wings must connect to the mineshaft.
Rooms in Wing 1: 2d4+3+hallways
Rooms in Each Wing: 2d4+hallways
NPCS: 4d6

Isolated Nature:
This setting type functions differently from the others. There isn't a map with rooms on it like the others have. Instead, as the players move around they encounter random areas. The players start at one of them, either rolled or determined by you.

1. Crashed Space Ship
2. Cliffs
3. Hill
4. Bunker
5. Forest
6. Lake
7. Strange Ruins
8. River

If this is an alien world you are encouraged to use various environmental effects such as low gravity or have the atmosphere being poison over the entirety of the planet. It is also advised that you consider the type of planet or nature this is. Is it a desert planet? A lush jungle? These are ultimately more important to the setting than the generated result.

Layout:
For 3 of the 4 setting types listed in this book the layout is up to you, but it should make sense, be straight forward and some-what compact. Place hallways to connect rooms where needed. There isn't really much need to make a full map, but it is helpful to know what rooms connect ot what.

Room Definitions:
Airlock:
- **Dimensions:** 10'x20'
- **Description:** This room has a port that leads out into space and only one door can be opened at a time.

Armory:
- **Dimensions:** 10'x10'
- **Description:** This room has 1d4 weapons and 1d3 body armors.

Barracks:
- **Dimensions:** 20'x40'
- **Description:** This room has a bunch of bunk beds and there are foot lockers at the beds which may have weapons and clothing in them.

Bathroom:
- **Dimensions:** 10'x10'
- **Description:** This room has a toilet and a sink.

Bedroom:
- **Dimensions:** 10'x20'
- **Description:** A mundane room. Has at least 1 bed.

Cargo Bay:
- **Dimensions:** 40'x40'
- **Description:** This room has whatever cargo was being carried or stored prior to the game.

Cockpit:
- **Dimensions:** 10'x10'
- **Description:** This room controls where the ship goes.

Common Room:
- **Dimensions:** 20'x30'
- **Description:** This is a mundane room with various tables, probably a microwave.

Courtyard:
- **Dimensions:** 40'x40'
- **Description:** An open space that might be open to the environment if the environment makes sense for that. Might have benches and the like.

Cryo Bay:
- **Dimensions:** 20'x30'
- **Description:** This room has cryo pods in it which suspend bio functions while active.

Engine Room:
- **Dimensions:** 10'x30'
- **Description:** This room controls the power to the facility.

Escape Pods:
- **Dimensions:** 10'x15'
- **Description:** This is a room that can disconnect from the main body of the facility. There are 2d3 escape pods which can hold either 1 or 2 people.

Freezer:
- **Dimensions:** 20'x20'
- **Description:** This room is heavily chilled. The cold deals 1 damage per round.

Furnace Room:
- **Dimensions:** 30'x30'
- **Description:** The heat in this room is not enough to deal damage unless the furnace is damaged, in which case it deals 1 damage per round. This room controls the heat and atmosphere of the facility.

Hanger:
- **Dimensions:** 30'x50'
- **Description:** This room has a large outside door and may hold vehicles.

Hallway:
- **Dimensions:** 5' to 10' wide.
- **Description:** Used to connect rooms.

Holding Cells:
- **Dimensions:** 5'x5' each
- **Description:** These rooms are locked by default and designed to keep a person inside of it. Rolls to unlock the door by force or picking are made a -5 total. There may be multiple holding cells as determined by you.

Kitchen:
- **Dimensions:** 20'x20'
- **Description:** This room is mundane and has various cooking tools such as knives, food and ovens.

Med Bay:
- **Dimensions:** 20'x30'
- **Description:** This room has a medical kit and grant +5 skill to medicine checks made while in that room.

Mine Shaft:
- **Dimensions:** 10'x100'
- **Description:** This "room" goes down at an angle, it's dark in there.

Office:
- **Dimensions:** 20'x20'
- **Description:** This room has a computer at a desk.

Science Lab:
- **Dimensions:** 20'x20'
- **Description:** This room has equipment in it that gives +5 skill to science based checks made while in that room.

Security Room:
- **Dimensions:** 10'x10'
- **Description:** This room has a security station which can view security cameras, which are in most of the rooms (you determine which ones) which it can watch as well as the ability to lock doors to rooms with electric locks. (you determine which ones have electric locks)

Sewers:
- **Dimensions:** 5' wide
- **Description:** Less of a room, this section goes under the facility. There is at least one entrance into the sewers from another room. If there is a trash disposal, bathroom, med bay or kitchen the sewers connect here. If there are none of these it connects to a hallway.

Supply Closet:
- **Dimensions:** 5'x5'
- **Description:** This is a small room with cleaning supplies.

Trash Disposal:
- **Dimensions:** 10'x10'
- **Description:** This room has a way of destroying objects which deals 2d10 damage if something or someone pushed into it. This can be fire, or physical depending on the type of disposal.

Vents:
- **Dimensions:** 5' wide
- **Description:** These are not so much a room, but a system throughout the facility above or between rooms. Each room has a 80% chance of having a vent port.

NPCs:

NPCs don't need anything beyond a name an a general expertise or lack there of. They don't have skills or statistics, instead they roll checks to do
something within their expertise as if their total was 14. Rolls for actions out of their expertise are rolled as if their total was 6. You don't even need to come up with all the NPCs for the setting, and can introduce them as they become relevant. It is a good idea to come up with a few important

NPCs before the game starts so that you have some names to throw out if needed.

Premise:
After all of that, you can generate the reason that the players are in the setting. Again, the chart rolled on is different based on which setting type is being used. These are more suggestions, much like this whole generation process.

Space Ship:
1. The players are sent in to kill, capture, or get samples of the alien.
2. The alien was already there in a hidden section and breaks out. The area is sealed off by those leaving outside.
3. Some-one brings in the alien secretly and it gets out.
4. A notice comes over the PA telling the players a biological contamination has been detected and exits are being sealed. The alien is loose, but the players don't know any-thing about it.
5. The players are transporting the alien and things go wrong. They have to get it back. They may or may not know what they are transporting.
6. The players start in cryo pods asleep (any androids are activated and wake up in the bay with them) with an alert coming over the intercom that "a biological contaminant has been detected." Throughout the ship there is some destruction. There is a 40% chance that an NPC was killed while every-one was asleep and a 30% chance that the person was in cryo when it happened.

Otherworld Colony:
1. The players are sent in to kill, capture, or get samples of the alien.
2. The alien was already there in a hidden section and breaks out. The area is sealed off by those leaving out-

side.
3. Some-one brings in the alien secretly and it gets out.
4. A notice comes over the PA telling the players a biological contamination has been detected and exits are being sealed. The alien is loose, but the players don't know any-thing about it.
5. The players are transporting the alien and things go wrong. They have to get it back. They may or may not know what they are transporting.
6. The players were sent in because there has been no contact with the area and the players are supposed to figure out why that is. The alien is already established and most or all the people there are dead, captured or hiding.

Asteroid Mining Facility:
1. The players are sent in to kill, capture, or get samples of the alien.
2. The alien was already there in a hidden section and breaks out. The area is sealed off by those leaving outside.
3-4. The players are transporting the alien and things go wrong. They have to get it back. They may or may not know what they are transporting.
5. Some-one brings in the alien secretly and it gets out.
6. A notice comes over the PA telling the players a biological contamination has been detected and exits are being sealed. The alien is loose, but the players don't know any-thing.

Isolated Nature:
1. The players are sent in to kill, capture, observe, or get samples of the alien in it's natural environment.
2. The players are transporting the alien and things go wrong. They have to get it back. They may or may not know what they are transporting.
3. The players were in a ship that encountered problems and had to make a crash landing on an unexplored planet. It can support life, but they haven't detected any.

...Yet.
4. The players are sent to collect some plant samples from a planet newly discovered to have life. When they are out getting samples, some-thing has damaged the ship and it will have to be repaired before they can leave.
5. The players are sent to survey a new planet. It's far enough out where it's a one way trip and they will be sending supplies via drone, as well as eventually sending other colonists.
6. It's been detected that there is some-kind of ruin on a far away world which can potentially hold life.

And you now have a setting and scenario. There is no official tech-level or cultural details created by this. Those are up to you. If you wish to keep all the games of Alien Outbreak for which you are Game Master within the same continuity that is up to you. If you don't want to go into any details, that is also fine but you'll probably have to make up some details such as what the asteroid is mining or if the fuel for space ships can be ignited, on the spot. At the end of this book, there are some pre-made materials to this effect if you wish to use one of those.

CHAPTER 7: The Structure of the Game

Alien Outbreak is broken into a three act structure. The acts flow as naturally from one to another with the only notable break in gameplay being at the third act. They function as a difficulty balance for the players, to keep the game from being too easy or impossible.

Act 1:
The first act is what gets the alien in with the players without a way out. It lasts from the start of the game until the first encounter with the alien. During the first act you should have something happen that either traps the players in the facility, such as their ship being damaged or needing to be refueled, or gives them a reason to stay, such as one of the player's kids going missing or having to obtain an item that is hidden. Most of the first act will be introducing the setting, NPCs and other details the players will be using throughout the rest of the game.

Act 2:
The second act is most of the game. It lasts from the end of the first act to as soon as the players figure out how they are going to deal with the alien and get out of there. Alternatively, it ends when the players give up on either of these. Throughout the second act, you keep track of a number called the "dynamic difficulty score," which measures how well the players have been doing throughout the game. The specifics of the dynamic difficulty score is discussed later on in this book. During this section, you should focus on keeping the players worried about the alien and on their toes. While there shouldn't be constant threat of death, there should be a constant threat of the threat of death. If you need to fudge the alien a bit to make it scary, this is the time to do it. Most character deaths that happen in the game should happen here.

Act 3:
The third act is a bit different. If they survive this long, it lasts from the end of the second act to the end of the game. At the start of the third act, the players spend the dynamic difficulty score on various positive or negative effects as discussed in that section. If the players try to flee the alien should chase after them. If the players are hunting down the alien, it should put up a fight. While most of the danger should be in the second act, the threat should still be there but it should be reactive to the players rather than proactive towards them.

The Dynamic Difficulty Score:
During the second act, you keep track of a score meant to measure how much trouble the players have run into or how well they have been doing. This score is hidden from the players until it is revealed at the start of the third act.
The score goes up by 1 from the following occurrences:
- Player death.
- Having to flee from the alien.
- An important piece of equipment being destroyed.
- Any situation which ends with the players as the clear loser or that causes a notable set back.
- The score goes down by 1 from the following occurrences:
- Killing an alien.
- If the alien has to flee to avoid dying.
- Rescuing a player that was captured by the alien.
- The players using meta-knowledge to get a leg up on the alien without having any reason to take those actions in-game.
- Any action that the players take that puts them at a clear advantage over the alien.

The score should change sparingly and shouldn't favor the players. If anything it should be biased against them.
At the start of the third act, the players must spend the dynamic difficulty score either down to 0 or up to 0. If the score is positive, the options they have to pick from are good

for them. If the score is negative, the options they have to pick from are bad for them. In the event that there are dead player characters, those players have a monopoly on how the score is spent.

Dynamic Difficulty Options:
You cannot select the same option multiple times unless the option says otherwise.

These options are also listed in the Player's Guide section of this book with different framing and levels of detail since they are not hidden to the players, but the rules on how the score is calculated are only in this book.

Positive Score:
- **3pts** - A dead player character managed to survive after all! They were probably hiding in the vents or something. They reenter play with half toughness but otherwise fine.
- **2pts** - A dead non-player character managed to survive after all! This functions the same as bringing back a player, but the GM has more control of it.
- **2pts** - There is a hidden weapons cache in the facility! It contains 2d3 weapons determined by the GM and is located in an area determined by the GM.
- **2pts** - One of the remaining scientist NPCs, or a scientist player, thinks they have a way to create a virus that specifically targets alien biology. This takes 1d4 hours of work in a lab, but when finished they have to make a theoretic science or they must spend an extra hour working before they can attempt the check again. When the virus is finished, it can be dispersed through the facilities vents or sewers or some-thing, where it deals 1 damage per minute to the alien until it dies. This cannot be selected if there are no scientists. If there are no vents or sewers, a dispersal unit can be built by an engineer. If there are no vents, sewers or engineers some-one will have to inject it into the alien or inject it into a person and have that person get eaten. If they chose this route, the injected

person takes 1 damage per minute. Androids do not take this damage from this but can deliver the virus.
- **1pts** - Outside help is on the way! They arrive in:
    [1] 1d4 days.
    [2] 1 day.
    [3] 3d6 hours.
    [4] 2d6 hours.
    Stat-wise it is 2d4 heavily armed rescue workers with expertise in firearms. They all have body armor and weapons.
- **1pts** - The alien's weakness is revealed! If the alien has a weakness the GM tells you what it is, otherwise the GM tells you what it's weakest attribute is.
- **1pts** - A player who was injured by the alien starts displaying the traits of the alien (if they were dead they come back to life), gaining a variation on one of the alien's traits, and gaining more as time progresses. They become very powerful, but when the use the alien's trait they have to roll a morale check or go berserk and starting attacking every-thing. Each round they can make another morale check to shake that off as a non-action. The alien is drawn to this player for the final confrontation.
- **1pts** - Someone found something! A player gets one item of their choice from the general items list or their class items list. You can select this option multiple times.
- **1pts** - The players get a second wind! Each player regains 1d4 toughness. A player can opt out to grant someone else their 1d4 of healing, but any given player can only regain 2d4 toughness from this option.
- **1pts** - Someone learned something! A player gains +1d4 to a skill of their choice. This option can be selected multiple times but only once per player.

Negative Score:
- **4pts** - Another type of alien shows up! Oh Boy! This one requires a pause in the game while the GM creates the new alien.
- **3pts** - The alien has reproduced.. Some how. There are

eggs 5d6 some-where which will hatch in 3d10 min. If there are any NPCs that are alive and not with the party, they show up and tell the players.
- **2pts** - Those killed by the alien come back to life under the control of the alien. They can use weapons and technology, but are not articulate or smart.
- **2pts** - The alien is converting the area into some-thing more suitable to it.

   [1] Fleshy cavelike area which is probably womb symbolism. (These tunnels are ripe for ambush against the players)

   [2] Superheating the area. (The area deals 1 damage per round to the people within, this does not affect the alien)

   [3] Flooding the area. (Fills the area with a fluid that the alien can breathe and swim through at normal speed. This does not expand by room, but by elevation)

   [4] Changing the atmosphere into a different composition. (The area becomes toxic as the poison trait)

   [5] Opening a portal to it's home dimension/timeline/some-thing and starting to merge the two. (Physics and time might function differently)

   [6] The alien is becoming the setting. (As the fleshy cavelike area, but the walls and floors make attacks. The alien is gone, but the area has it's traits and uses it's statistics). The area changed expands by a room or so every few minutes.
- **2pts** - The alien is too dangerous to escape, one of the NPCs is found to have destroyed all the exits, ways out, and communication with the outside world to seal the alien in.
- **1pts** - Destruction! Part (2d4 rooms, 2d6 if a large facility) of the facility is destroyed and inaccessible. This could be from acid, void, fire, etc.
- **1pts** - Power trouble! The power in the facility goes out. The backup power needs to be activated manually in an appropriate room with either a mechanical or electrical check depending on the nature of the damage.
- **1pts** - A storm is brewing. In 4d6 minutes, a massive

storm will hit, being outside in the storm deals 1d6 damage per round. While inside, power loss in certain rooms may occur, certain rooms may collapse and it is loud enough where being in a room that shares an exterior wall causes -5 to perception skills and checks.
- **1pts** - A player who was injured or killed by the alien starts displaying the traits of the alien (If they were dead they come back to life), gaining one of the alien's traits, and gaining more as time progresses. They become very powerful, but when the use the alien's trait they have to roll a morale check or go berserk and starting attacking every-thing. Each round they can make another morale check to shake that off. The alien is drawn to this player for the final confrontation and can be easily ambushed. If they were killed by the alien, that player still controls them but they are working with the alien now.
- **1pts** - Outside forces (Government, "the company", etc) have decided to nuke the whole place from afar. The players are tasked with containing the alien so it gets killed in the blast.

PART 3:
Samples and Ready-Mades

CHAPTER 8: Sample Aliens

Sample Aliens:
This section is to provide samples of aliens both in order to allow you to double check if your alien seems to be reasonable, but also for examples that you can use on the fly if you are pressed for time. Some of these aliens were hand designed rather than generated and a couple of them are specific references to movie or book aliens. Feel free to use these as much as you want, but the game generally works best when you create your own.

Gravoid:

This alien is on the weaker side and is the alien made for use in the ready-made game.

Infant:

Appearance: A cat sized inky black lump with a number of small eyes covering the main mass. Four multi-jointed legs extend down from the body and just seem to end in stumps. The joints in it's legs seem to shift place as it moves.

Toughness: 2
Special: 23
Strength: 13
Instinct: 17
Speed: 42: 90'

Basic Attack: <17, 1d8+2, grab<10

Traits:
- **Unpredictable Movement:** If any attacks miss the alien it moves 5' in a direction of it's choice and regains a special point.
- **Multistage Lifeform:** The alien has 3 stages of life. A newborn is 2 sizes smaller and only has the unpredictable movement trait. An adolescent has all the traits but one and is 1 size smaller. The adult is the alien as normal. It takes 4 hours to mature to the next stage after birth and the adult is the only form in which it can reproduce.

Weakness:
- **Odd Appetite:** Needs to consume some kind of odd material as food - steel/metal.

Structure:
- **Quadroped:** Has 4 legs.
- **No Arms:** Has no arms.

Tiny: +20 speed, -10 strength and toughness.

Cheating:
- **Staggered Turn:** If the alien has multiple actions it rolls initiative for each action beyond the first.

Adolescent:

Appearance: A dog sized inky black lump with a number of small eyes covering the main mass. On the bottom of this mass there is what at first seems to be a hand sized spike, but it is quickly revealed to be some kind of beak. Four multi-jointed legs extend down from the body and just seem to end in stumps. The joints in it's legs seem to shift place as it moves.

Toughness: 12
Special: 23
Strength: 23
Instinct: 17
Speed: 32: 65'

Beak: <17, 1d8+4, chunk <10
Basic Attack: <17, 1d4+4, grab<10

Traits:
- **Beak:** The alien has a beak, instead of grabbing with it's basic attack on a roll of 10 or less it bites out a chunk of them, and the damage dealt with that attack cannot be healed.
- **Unpredictable Movement:** If any attacks miss the alien it moves 5' in a direction of it's choice and regains a special point.
- **Multistage Lifeform:** The alien has 3 stages of life. A newborn is 2 sizes smaller and only has the unpredictable movement trait. An adolescent has all the traits but one and is 1 size smaller. The adult is the alien as normal. It takes 4 hours to mature to the next stage after birth and

the adult is the only form in which it can reproduce.

Weakness:
- **Odd Appetite:** Needs to consume some kind of odd material as food - steel/metal.

Structure:
- **Quadroped:** Has 4 legs.
- **No Arms:** Has no arms.

Small: +10 speed, -5 strength and toughness.

Cheating:
- **Staggered Turn:** If the alien has multiple actions it rolls initiative for each action beyond the first.

Fully Grown:

Appearance: A man sized inky black lump with a number of small eyes covering the main mass. On the bottom of this mass there is what at first seems to be a spike the length of your forearm, but it is quickly revealed to be some kind of beak. Four multi-jointed legs extend down from the body and just seem to end in stumps. The joints in it's legs seem to shift place as it moves. Standing with it's legs fully extended, it is nearly 8' in height, with the beak hanging down at about head level.

Toughness: 17
Special: 23
Strength: 28
Instinct: 17
Speed: 22: 40'

Beak: <17, 1d8+5, chunk<10
Basic Attack: <17, 1d8+5, grab<10

Traits:
- **Beak:** The alien has a beak, instead of grabbing with it's basic attack on a roll of 10 or less it bites out a chunk of them, and the damage dealt with that attack cannot be healed.
- **Unpredictable Movement:** If any attacks miss the alien it moves 5' in a direction of it's choice and regains a special point.
- **Multistage Lifeform:** The alien has 3 stages of life. A newborn is 2 sizes smaller and only has the unpredictable movement trait. An adolescent has all the traits but one and is 1 size smaller. The adult is the alien as normal. It takes 4 hours to mature to the next stage after birth and the adult is the only form in which it can reproduce.

Weakness:
- **Odd Appetite:** Needs to consume some kind of odd material as food - steel/metal.

Structure:
- **Quadroped:** Has 4 legs.
- **No Arms:** Has no arms.

Medium: No modifiers.

Cheating:
- **Staggered Turn:** If the alien has multiple actions it rolls initiative for each action beyond the first.

Exosoman:

Appearance: The creature hanging from the ceiling looks like a man whose skin is the shell of a beetle. His head is elongated with large empty eyes and a fleshy razor sharp tail swings behind him menacingly.

Drone:

Toughness: 22
Special: 16
Strength: 26
Instinct: 24
Speed: 17: 30'

Basic Attack: <24, 1d8+5, grab<10
Razor Tail: <24, 1d8+5, impale<10

Traits:
- **Acid Blood:** When it takes damage it sprays acid blood that hits all adjacent targets, forcing an agility check or they take 1d6 damage, and melts through various things.
- **Razor Tail:** The alien can make an attack with it's tail that deals 1d8+1/5th strength. On a roll of 10 or less, he impales the target on the tail, requiring a stength check to escape from. It can spend 2 special points to add this effect to a result of 12 or less after the roll has been made.
- **Climbing:** Can climb at the same rate it can run.
- **Dark-vision:** Can see in the dark.
- **Leap:** The alien can jump as high and far as it can move in a turn without having to roll.

Weakness:
- **Weak to Fire or Cold:** Takes double damage from fire.

Behavior:
- **Queen and Drones:** There is one queen who births a

large brood of 4d6 aliens every once in a while. The queen is automatically Huge and has 1/2 speed of her brood.
- **Capture:** The alien will attempt to single out and capture creatures and bring them to an isolated spot to eat in piece.

Structure:
- **Biped:** Has 2 legs, +1 speed.
- **Arms:** The alien has arms and can hold things. Each arm grants +1 str. Has 2 arms.
- **Head:** Has a head separate from it's body and gains +2 instinct.

Size: Medium: About the size of a human being, 5-8'. No modifiers.

Reproduction:
- **Reproduction Attack:** Can reproduce with a special ovipositor attack that deals 1d6 damage and costs 2 special points. The reproduction ends with the birth of 1 egg. After getting impregnated, the player must make a morale check or feel the need to protect the eggs because they are their children. NPCs automatically fail this check. Only the queen can use the ovipositer attack.

Cheating:
- **Cheat Death:** If there is only one alien, or one alien left, it does not die and continues to plague the players at inconvient moments. Alternatively, this is the "there was another one" trope, where you kill the alien only to surprise them with a second one later on.

Queen:
Has identical traits, weaknesses, behaviors, structure, reproduction and cheating.

Toughness: 37

Special: 16
Strength: 41
Instinct: 24
Speed: 3; 5'

Basic Attack: <24, 1d8+8, grab<10
Razor Tail: <24, 1d8+8, impale<10
Ovipositor: <24, 1d6+8

Size: Huge: About the size of an elephant or larger, 16'-25'. -10 speed, +15 strength and toughness. Can make melee attacks from 10' away.

Salt Pillar

Appearance: This huge pillar-like creature has cracked papery skin and a set of eyes at about 8' up. While it stands on two legs like a human, it is missing any arms. Each step it takes is slow but large. The very air around is dry as dust and bits of static arc around it as it shifts in place.

Toughness: 45
Special: 16
Strength: 40
Instinct: 27
Speed: 17: 15'+(1d6*5)'

Basic Attack: <27, can attack at up to 10', 1d8+8+corrupting influence, grab<10
Dust: 2sp, 1d4 agility after 1d3rds, 1/hour until proper surgery
Static Buildup: 10'/move action, 1d4

Traits:
- **Lurching:** Reduce movement speed by 1/2, but whenever it moves roll 1d6 and move an additional amount of 5' increments equal to the roll.
- **Dust:** The alien can spend a special point to spew out a 20' cloud of dust which reduces agility by 1d4 to all within the dust after 1d3 rounds and deals that damage once per hour until it has been removed through a successful surgery attempt after properly studying the dust with theoretical science.
- **Aura:** The alien has an aura of static electricity that deals 1 damage per 5' moved through. The aura goes out 15'.
- **Corrupting Influence:** Interacting with the alien causes the alien's influence to spread. This requires a successful attack, and if affected the creature starts to show symptoms after 2d6 hours. The symptoms, once they manifest, are losing 1d4 morale and the victim must make a morale check to take an action that goes against the

alien.
- **Static Buildup:** As the alien moves, it acrues static electricity which it can discharge as a ranged attack dealing 1d4 with a range of 10' per number of actions spent to move.

Weakness:
Charge Up: The alien starts with 0 special points, but can have an amount of points equal to the amount rolled for the special stat. It gains 2 special points which last for 1 minute whenever it takes damage.

Structure:
- **Biped:** has 2 legs, +1 speed
- **Head:** has a head separate from it's body and gains +2 instinct.

Large: -5 speed, +10 strength and toughness, can make melee attacks from 5' farther away than normal.

Behavior:
- **Grudge:** the alien will go after whoever hurts it first with an infinite vengeance.

Reproduction:
- **Does not Reproduce:** the alien cannot reproduce.

Cheating:
- **Wound Points:** Instead of taking damage the alien gets wounds. If it

is hit by an attack that would deal 4 or more damage it gets a wound, it can sustain a number of wounds equal to 1/4 its toughness. If hit by an attack that would deal less than 4 damage it is a "glancing blow" that has no effect.

The Hunter

Appearance: This thin creature stands on two legs which take up a large portion of it's height. Around it's body, there are various pouches and pieces of tech. Of note, on his shoulder there is a large cyllindrical object, which starts to hum and glow before shooting a blast of energy at you.

Toughness: 18 (Body Armor 10)
Special: 19
Strength: 16
Instinct: 27
Speed: 19; 35'
Intelligence: 20

Basic Attack: <27, 1d8+, grab<10
Razor Disk: <27, 1d6, 20'
Shoulder Gun: <27, 2d6, 60'

Traits:
- **Sapient [2]:** Has an intelligence score rolled the same way as the rest of the statistics which is used for the alien's reasoning and in place of skills that the players would use intelligence for, starts with the following weapons:
- A razor sharp thrown disc with a range of 20' that deals 1d6 damage but can sticks in the target it. Can be set as a trap that floats in the air or sticks to a wall and attacks when it detects motion that is not the alien within it's range.
- A shoulder mounted gun which deals 2d6 and has a range of 60' the alien can get which makes an attack each round without spending an action.
- It has body armour. Any attacks with equipment cost 1 special point.
- **Invisibility:** Cannot be directly detected visibly. Must spend 1 special point per round to maintain the invisibility.

- **Traps:** Can set traps for 2 special points which need a perception check to be noticed. A net or glue trap which requires an agility check to escape.

Weakness:
- **Limited Vision:** Can only see infared.

Behavior:
- **Sapient Intelligence:** The alien is as smart or smarter than humans and is from a species that has technology and can understand tech after spending a few minutes with it. It is smart, will set traps, and values it's own life. They may or may not be armed and have equipment.

Structure:
- **Biped:** Has 2 legs, +1 speed.
- **Arms:** The alien has arms and can hold things. Each arm grants +1 str. Has 3 arms.

Medium: About the size of a human being, 5-8'. No modifiers.

Reproduction:
- **Sexual Reproduction:** 2 aliens are required to reproduce.

Cheating:
- **Meta Knowledge:** Assume that the alien knows all of the actions of the players, even if the alien has no way of knowing that information.

Space Hedge:

Appearance: A tangled mess of greenish tubes that intersect each other without converging on a central mass that you can determine. The mass rears back into what seems to be some kind of runner's stance.

Toughness: 21
Special: 24
Strength: 20
Instinct: 23
Speed: 25; 50'

Basic Attack: <23, 1d8+4, grab<10

Traits:
- **Charge:** If the alien moves before making an attack, they add +1 to the damage per 10' moved. If the alien only has one action it can move up to 1/2 it's speed and make an attack as a single action.
- **Plant Cells:** When the alien takes more than 5 damage from a single attack, part of it's body is severed. Even a single cell of the alien can grow into a full alien. The body parts start at 5hp and grow 1 hp per minute. As they gain hp they grow in size until they are the full alien. Partly grown aliens can act, but are pathetic enough where they don't need to be fully stated out but still have the traits of the alien.
- **Can Live in Space:** The vacuum and cold of space do not harm it.

Structure:
- **More than Four Legs:** 8 legs, for every 2 legs above 2 it gets +2 speed.
- **Arms:** The alien has arms and can hold things. 2 arms. Each arm grants +1 str.

Medium: no modifiers

Behavior:
- **Cyclical:** the alien only needs to eat 3 things before it goes back into a hibernation state for many years

Stone Dog:

Appearance: A bulky dog-like creature with sharp front talons that and to be made out of stone and has a number of holes pocketing it's body, a black oily liquid leaking out of them. A closer look shows that there are small centipedal bugs crawling around in the liquid. It eyes [player] intensely.

Toughness: 31
Special: 18
Strength: 16
Instinct: 24
Speed: 18: 30'

Claws: <24, 1d6+3, twice as action
Roar: 30', force morale check, 1d6 morale damage
Acid Blood: If hit force agility check, all adjacent, 1d6
Basic Attack: <24, 1d8+3, grab<10

Traits:
- **Roar:** The alien can spend 1 special point to let out a blood chilling roar that deals 1d6 morale damage if people within 30' of it fail a morale check.
- **Regeneration:** Heals 4 damage at the start of each round.
- **Symbiotes:** The alien has tiny symbiotes living in it. When it makes it's bite attack or takes damage from a melee attack the target has to roll an agility check or some symbiotes are transferred to the target. These symbiotes effect humans differently from how they affect the alien. The alien can detect and track the symbiotes and effectively knows where any hosts are at all times.
- **Acid Blood:** When it takes damage it sprays acid blood that hits all adjacent targets and melts through various things.
- **Mineral:** The alien has a mineral structure rather than an animal structure. It is immune to chemical compounds

that affect living creatures (poison, medicine, etc), does not count as alive, and gets +10 toughness.
- **Oily Secretions:** The alien secretes an oil by spending 1 special point (it takes an action to start secreting, but does not take an action to maintain secreting it. It costs 1 special point per round it is active). The oil is slippery and requires an agility check to move through without falling over.
- **Claws:** Can make 2 claw attacks as a single action that deal 1d6+1/5th strength.

Structure:
- **No Arms:** has no arms and gains +2 speed.
- **Quadroped:** has 4 legs, +2 speed.

Medium: no modifiers.

Behavior:
- **Pack:** There are 5 aliens and they hunt as a group.

Cheating:
- **Focused Targeting:** The alien "picks on" a particular player determined randomly and will target them more than 1/2 the time.
- **Staggered Turn:** If the alien has multiple actions it rolls initiative for each action beyond the first.

Zigg-Zalio:

Newborn:

Appearance: This creature is somewhat crab-like in shape and about the size of a large dog, with six legs and two small arms ending in pincers. It has two extremely large heads, each with a single eye and large mouth connected to the body by a thick neck. As you are looking at it, the space around it warps and seems almost to reverse for a moment. That was probably just your imagination.

Strength: 18
Toughness: 17
Instinct: 25
Speed: 30: 60'
Special: 16

Basic Attack: <25, 1d8+5, >10 grab

Traits:
- **Dimension Hopping:** Can spend 4 special points to shift in or out of this reality into a different plane. It can pull people and objects through with it. This plane of reality is. The reality overlaps in certain areas (as the first result, but only in certain rooms). The reality is a "reverse reality" from the normal reality. Direction is reversed.

Structure:
- **More than Four Legs:** For every 2 legs above 2 it gets +2 speed. 6 legs
- **Arms:** The alien has arms and can hold things. Each arm grants +1 str. 2 arms
- **x2 Head:** has a head separate from it's body and gains +2 instinct.

Small: About the size of a medium sized dog, 3'-5'. +10 speed, -5 strength and toughness.

Behavior:
- **Nesting:** The alien creates a hidden nest where it will generally hang around.
- **Capture:** The alien will attempt to single out and capture other creatures and bring them to an isolated spot to eat in piece.

Reproduction:
- **Multistage Life-Form:** The alien has 3 stages of life. A newborn is 2 sizes smaller and only has 1 of the traits of the alien. An adolescent has all the traits but one and is 1 size smaller. The adult is the alien as normal. It takes 4 hours to mature to the next stage after birth and the adult is the only form in which it can reproduce, which it does as per sexual reproduction.

Cheating:
- **Secret Notes:** Pass out notes to the players at various times throughout the game. The content of these notes can be details that only they see or just dummy notes to make people nervous. Feel free to use this to turn players against each other by lying about details as well.

Adolescent:

Appearance: This creature is somewhat crab-like in shape and about the size of a lion, with six legs and two small arms ending in pincers. Spines cover most of it's body. It has two extremely large heads, each with a single eye and large mouth connected to the body by a thick neck. As you are looking at it, the space around it warps and seems almost to reverse for a moment. That was probably just your imagination.

Strength: 23

Toughness: 21
Instinct: 25
Speed: 20; 35'
Special: 16

Basic Attack: <25, 1d8+6, >10 grab

Traits:
- **Dimension Hopping:** Can spend 4 special points to shift in or out of this reality into a different plane. It can pull people and objects through with it. This plane of reality is. The reality overlaps in certain areas (as the first result, but only in certain rooms). The reality is a "reverse reality" from the normal reality. Direction is reversed.
- **Swallow Whole:** The alien can eat any-one it grabs with it's mouth as an action by making another attack roll against the grabbed person. If it succeeds, the grabbed person is eaten; they remain alive but take 1d4 damage each round and the only action they can take is to make a strength check to escape.
- **Charge:** If the alien moves before making an attack, they add +1 to the damage per 10' moved. If the alien only has one action it can move up to 1/2 it's speed and make an attack as a single action.
- **Spines:** The alien is covered in spines. When a melee attack is made against the alien, the attacker must roll agility or take 1d4 damage. The alien's melee attacks deal an extra 2 damage.

Structure:
- **More than Four Legs:** For every 2 legs above 2 it gets +2 speed. 6 legs
- **Arms:** The alien has arms and can hold things. Each arm grants +1 str. 2 arms
- **x2 Head:** has a head separate from it's body and gains +2 instinct.

Medium: No modifiers

Behavior:
- **Nesting:** The alien creates a hidden nest where it will generally hang around.
- **Capture:** The alien will attempt to single out and capture other creatures and bring them to an isolated spot to eat in piece.

Reproduction:
- **Multistage Life-Form:** The alien has 3 stages of life. A newborn is 2 sizes smaller and only has 1 of the traits of the alien. An adolescent has all the traits but one and is 1 size smaller. The adult is the alien as normal. It takes 4 hours to mature to the next stage after birth and the adult is the only form in which it can reproduce, which it does as per sexual reproduction.

Cheating:
- **Secret Notes:** Pass out notes to the players at various times throughout the game. The content of these notes can be details that only they see or just dummy notes to make people nervous. Feel free to use this to turn players against each other by lying about details as well.

Fully Grown:

Appearance: This creature is somewhat crab-like in shape and considerably larger than a horse, with six legs and two small arms ending in pincers. Spines cover most of it's body. It has two extremely large heads, each with a single eye and large mouth connected to the body by a thick neck. As you are looking at it, the space around it warps and seems almost to reverse for a moment. That was probably just your imagination.

Strength: 33
Toughness: 31

Instinct: 25
Speed: 15; 25'
Special: 16

Basic Attack: <25, 1d8+8, >10 grab

Traits:
- **Dimension Hopping:** Can spend 4 special points to shift in or out of this reality into a different plane. It can pull people and objects through with it. This plane of reality is. The reality overlaps in certain areas (as the first result, but only in certain rooms). The reality is a "reverse reality" from the normal reality. Direction is reversed.
- **Swallow Whole:** The alien can eat any-one it grabs with it's mouth as an action by making another attack roll against the grabbed person. If it succeeds, the grabbed person is eaten; they remain alive but take 1d4 damage each round and the only action they can take is to make a strength check to escape.
- **Charge:** If the alien moves before making an attack, they add +1 to the damage per 10' moved. If the alien only has one action it can move up to 1/2 it's speed and make an attack as a single action.
- **Spines**: The alien is covered in spines. When a melee attack is made against the alien, the attacker must roll agility or take 1d4 damage. The alien's melee attacks deal an extra 2 damage.

Structure:
- **More than Four Legs:** For every 2 legs above 2 it gets +2 speed. 6 legs
- **Arms:** The alien has arms and can hold things. Each arm grants +1 str. 2 arms
- **x2 Head:** has a head separate from it's body and gains +2 instinct

Large: About the size of a mid-sized car, 9'-15'-5 speed, +10 strength and toughness. Can make melee attacks from 10' away.

Behavior:
- **Nesting:** The alien creates a hidden nest where it will generally hang around.
- **Capture:** The alien will attempt to single out and capture other creatures and bring them to an isolated spot to eat in piece.

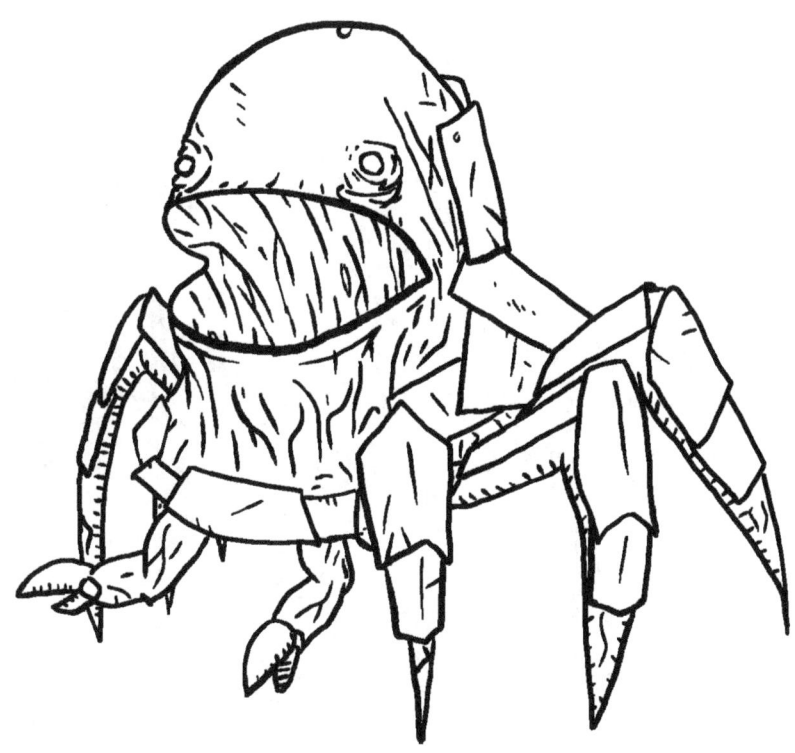

Reproduction:
- **Multistage Life-Form:** The alien has 3 stages of life. A newborn is 2 sizes smaller and only has 1 of the traits of the alien. An adolescent has all the traits but one and is 1 size smaller. The adult is the alien as normal. It takes 4 hours to mature to the next stage after birth and the adult is the only form in which it can reproduce, which it does as per sexual reproduction.

Cheating:
- **Secret Notes:** Pass out notes to the players at various times throughout the game. The content of these notes can be details that only they see or just dummy notes to make people nervous. Feel free to use this to turn players against each other by lying about details as well.

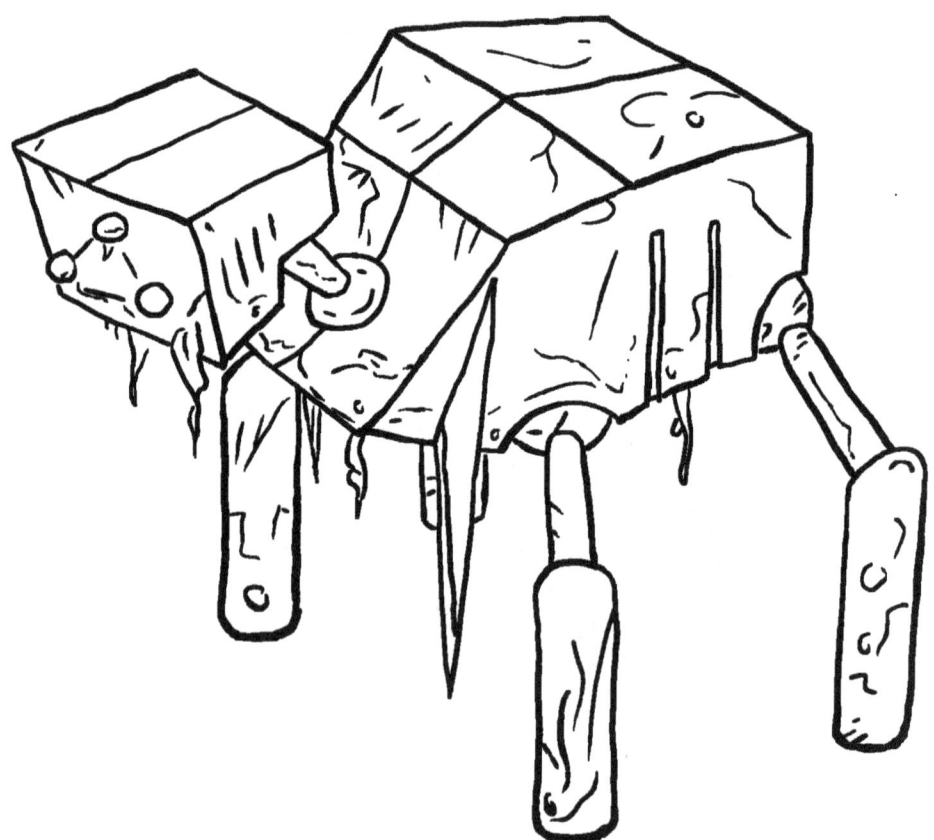

The Blade Beast:

Appearance: A giant metal creature nearly the size of a house with multiple razor-sharp blades jutting out from it like swords. As it moves, the ground shakes its metal legs grind on each other loudly. On its head, 3 orbs that might be eyes glow red as it turns towards you.

Strength: 33
Toughness: 42
Instinct: 21
Speed: 13: 20'
Special: 10

Basic Attack: <21, 1d8+6, >10grab
Blades: 2 attacks as an action, <21, 1d6+6, >10 1 ongoing damage

Traits:
- **Robotic:** The alien is non-biological. Checks involving knowledge of the alien are made as mechanical checks rather than biology checks. The alien can repair itself by taking pieces of mechanical equipment and grafting them onto their body. This takes 2d6 minutes and heals 2d6 hp. It can also refill its special pool in the same way.
- **Natural Armor:** Takes 5 less damage per attack taken.
- **Blades:** The alien has 2 long razor sharp blades somewhere on it's body which it can make attacks with a single action. It can be either organic bone blades or metal blades implanted on it. It can make a number of attacks equal to the number of blades it has. Each blade deals 1d6 damage and on a roll of 10 or less cause the target to take 1 damage per round until they are cured by a surgery check which takes 1 round. The alien can spend 3 special points to grow another blade that lasts for 1 minute.
- **Drone Body:** The alien is a featureless blob incapable of defending itself, but controls a more dangerous body re-

motely. The remote body is what is rolled up for alien creation, while the blob has 0strength, 10 toughness, instinct equal to the remote body, 7 speed, 0 special and is tiny sized. If the helpless body is killed the remote body is as well, but not the other way around. The remote body is expendable and can be "repaired" by the helpless body at a rate of 1d8 toughness per 10 minutes.

Weakness:
- **Staggerable:** The alien takes penalties on rolls from damage in the same way that a human would.
- **Loud:** The alien either emits some sort of noise, moves loudly or otherwise announces it's presence before it actually shows up.

Structure:
- **Head:** has a head separate from it's body and gains +2 instinct.
- **Quadruped:** Has 4 legs, +2 speed.

Huge: About the size of an elephant or larger, 16'-25'. -10 speed, +15 strength and toughness. Can make melee attacks from 10' away.

Behavior:
- **Searching:** The alien is searching for a particular object or artifact which is up to you to decide what it is and why the alien is after it. Once it finds and obtains this object it will try to escape with it.
- **Rampage:** Once the alien starts fighting, it does not stop.

Reproduction:
- **Sexual Reproduction:** 4 aliens are required to reproduce. This process takes 2 hours and yields 1d6 aliens. The aliens cannot reproduce for another 2d10 hours. The aliens born are eggs that hatch after 2d4 hours.

Mind-ipede:

Appearance: This creature like a strange fleshy centipede covered in scabs. As it moves, there is almost a stutter around it; as if some of the steps it was taking weren't actually happening.

Strength: 14
Toughness: 11
Instinct: 14
Speed: 32: 65'
Special: 22

Skills:
- **Attack:** 19
- **Stealth:** 4
- **Sense Motive:** 9

Basic Attack: <14, 1d8+2, >10 grab
Mind Control: instinct vs intelligence

Traits:
- **Sixth Sense:** The alien cannot be ambushed and, on the first round of combat, gets 1.5 times the number of actions it would normally get.
- **Scabs:** When damaged the alien develops 1 scab per time injured 1d4 minutes later. These scabs have 2 toughness and take damage first as body armor. Scabs that take damage do not develop scabs.
- **Psychic Powers:** Has psychic abilities that it can spend special points to use: Mind Control. (instinct vs intelligence attack, takes 5 rounds to recharge per attack and an additional round per minute of successful control)
- **Strange Time:** The alien interacts strangely with time. The alien can "undo" events affecting it for 4 special points. (This is mainly attacks against it but could be things such as trackers being put on it and the like as

well. It does not include things that do not directly physically affect it such as the players gaining information on it or seeing it)
- **Minions:** Has weaker aliens that help it, there are 6 of them and they have 15 on each stat and 1 trait. They treat the main alien as more important than itself. They have a bite/generic melee attack that deals 1d4+1/5 strength.

Structure:
- **More than Four Legs:** For every 2 legs above 2 it gets +2 speed. 7 legs.
- **No Arms:** Has no arms and gains +2 speed.

Small: About the size of a medium sized dog, 3'-5'. +10 speed, -5 strength and toughness.

Behavior:
- **Sapient Intelligence:** The alien is as smart or smarter than humans and is from a species that has technology and can understand tech after spending a few minutes with it. It is smart, will set traps, and values it's own life.

Reproduction:
- **Sexual Reproduction:** 2 aliens are required to reproduce. This process takes 1d4 hours and yields 1d4 aliens. The aliens cannot reproduce for another 1d8 days. The aliens born are eggs that hatch after 2d4 hours.

Cheating:
- **Skills:** The alien has a number of skill points equal to twice its instinct score+10. It's skills are: attack, stealth, secondary movement(climb, fly, etc), sense motive. The skill points are distributed by a priority system. Roll a d10 for each skill that the alien could end up using; the highest roll gets 1/2 the skill points, the second highest gets 1/2 the remaining, the third highest gets 1/2 the remaining and so forth.
- **Recharge Abilities:** Instead of spending special points

to use abilities, the aliens abilities are on a timer of their special point cost number of rounds after each use before they can be used again. The alien loses the "special" ability score.

Minion:

Appearance: This lump of flesh does not really have any distinct shape, features, or structure. It seems to be gathering up pieces of debris and other small objects as it rolls around the room.

Body: 31
Cunning: 15
Special: 15

Basic Attack: <15, 1d3+6, >10 grab

Trait:
- **Accrue:** The alien can spend 1 special point to absorb organic matter into itself, increasing it's toughness by 1d4. If the matter or parts can resist, they get a toughness roll to do so. For every 5 things it absorbs it grows in size by 1. (It does not gain any additional body for the size increases however)

Weakness:
- **Low Damage:** The aliens attacks deal 1 die step less. (1d8 to 1d6, 1d6 to 1d4, 1d4 to 1d3, 1d3 to 1)

Structure:
- **No Legs:** Has no legs and takes -4 speed, but gets +6 toughness.
- **No Arms:** Has no arms and gains +2 speed.

Large: About the size of a mid-sized car, 9'-15'-5 speed, +10 strength and toughness. Can make melee attacks from 10' away.

Reproduction:
- **Asexual Reproduction:** Can reproduce without other aliens.

Cheating:
- **Condensed Statistics Block:** The alien's toughness and strength are combined into an attribute called Body. Body is equal to the higher of strength or toughness. Speed and instinct are similarly combined into a stat called Cunning.

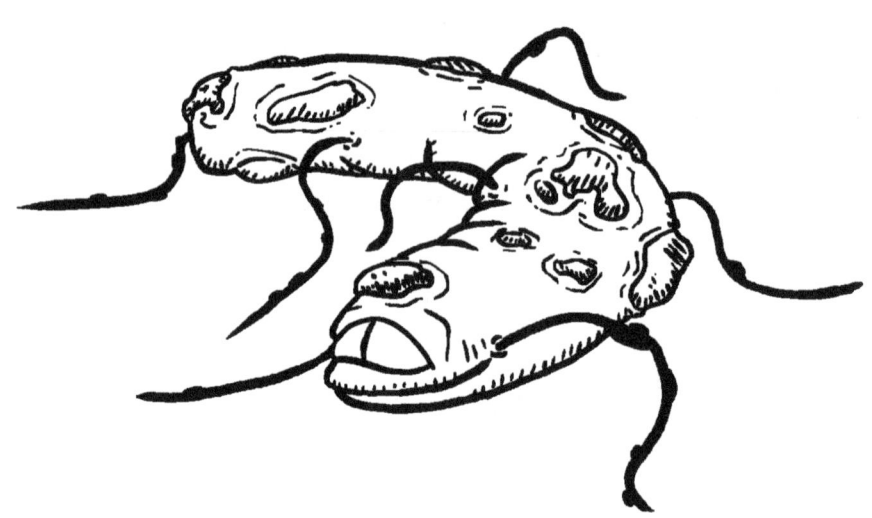

Venom-Tongue:

Appearance: As this creature flickers into view, you see it retracting a long wet tongue back into it's wide grinning mouth. It's body is bipedal with two arms but it has no head. It's skin is covered in lumpy and uneven scales. Then, it vanishes again.

Strength: 19
Toughness: 20
Instinct: 26
Speed: 17: 35'
Special: 11

Basic Attack: <26, 1d8ish+3+poison, >10 grab
Tongue: <26, pull 10'

Traits:
- **Tongue:** The alien has a long tongue 10' long. It is sticky and can be used as an attack that pulls you 10' towards the alien if it hits.
- **Poison:** One of it's attacks has a poison on it, when it hits and deals damage the poison takes effect after the encounter ends. The poison lasts until cured with a medicine check. The poison causes hallucinations for 1d6 minutes 1 round after exposure.
- **Invisibility:** Cannot be directly detected visibly. Must spend 1 special point per round to use.

Weakness:
- **Low Statistic:** Reduce toughness by half.
- **Fear:** The alien is afraid of fire.

Structure:
- **Biped:** Has 2 legs, +1 speed.
- **Arms:** The alien has arms and can hold things. Each arm grants +1 str. Has 2 arms.

Medium: About the size of a human being, 5-8'. No modifiers.

Behavior:
- **Play with your Food:** The alien will torture their prey and some-times let them go to hunt them later.

Reproduction:
- **Sexual Reproduction:** 5 aliens are required to reproduce. This process takes 4 hours and yields 1 alien. The aliens cannot reproduce for another 12 days. The aliens born are live birth.

Cheating:
- **Weird Dice:** Whenever the alien rolls a die or dice, roll a die or dice of your choosing. This can change throughout the game.

Blood Star:

Appearance: This creature is very similar to a starfish, but is about three feet in diameter. A small opening in the middle appears to have some sort of appendage moving around inside it. It is floating a few feet off the ground and starts wiggling at you menacingly.

Strength: 7
Toughness: 12
Instinct: 21
Speed: 26: 50'
Special: 18

Basic Attack: <21, 1d6+1, >10 grab+parasite
Mind Thrust: 2sp <21, 1d8+4
Mind Control: 5sp+1sp/minute, instinct vs. intelligence

Traits:
- **Parasite:** The alien is a parasite. It can crawl into/onto it's host if it grabs some-thing with it's bite attack where it dwells and slowly kills it's host, dealing 1d4 damage per hour. If you try to remove it, it requires a theory check to figure out how the alien is attached, then a biology check at -15 skill to remove. It deals 1d8 damage when removed. This defaults the alien to tiny size. The alien grows as it damages it's host and each hour it is on a person it grows 1 size and it's stats are adjusted. Once it reaches small size it detaches upon which it loses the parasite trait.
- **Psychic Powers:** Has psychic abilities that it can spend special points to use.
- **Mind Thrust.** (instinct based attack, range 30', 1d8+1/5th instinct damage to morale, costs 2 special points)
- **Mind Control.** (instinct vs intelligence attack, costs 5 special points per attack and per minute)
- **Track by Thought.** (can detect thoughts of things within 60' by spending 2 special points)

- **Regeneration:** Heals 1 damage at the start of each round.
- **Corrupting Influence:** Interacting with the alien causes the alien's influence to spread. This requires contact with the alien. Any method of the affecting a non-alien allows the affected creature a morale check to resist. After affected, the creature starts to show symptoms after 2d6 hours. The symptoms, once they manifest, are losing 1d4 morale and the victim must make a morale check to take an action that goes against the alien.
- **Flight:** Can fly at the same rate it can move across the ground.

Weakness:
- **Low Damage:** The aliens attacks deal 1 die step less. (1d8 to 1d6, 1d6 to 1d4, 1d4 to 1d3, 1d3 to 1)

Structure:
- **Arms:** The alien has arms and can hold things. Each arm grants +1 str. 1 arm.
- **No Legs:** Has no legs and takes -4 speed, but gets +6 toughness.

Tiny: About the size of a house cat, 1'-3'. +20 speed, -10 strength and toughness.

Behavior:
- **Sapient Intelligence:** The alien is as smart or smarter than humans and is from a species that has technology and can understand tech after spending a few minutes with it. It is smart, will set traps, and values it's own life. They may or may not be armed and have equipment.

Reproduction:
- **Asexual Reproduction:** Can reproduce without other aliens.

Cheating:
- **Skin Suit:** One of the NPCS is actually the alien in disguise as a human. It doesn't really matter if this makes sense or not since it should be a surprise sometime in Act 2 or 3.

CHAPTER 9: Sample Scenarios

Sample Scenarios:
As with the sample alien sections this sections is mainly for comparative use or quick play. It is worth noting that, even though some of these includes one, it is not required to create a scaled map but it is a good idea to have a general idea of the layout. All of these scenarios are intentionally over-built so that they are able to be picked up and played without the GM having to fill in any gaps. They provide a lot more detail than is actually needed and GMs are advised to improvise when running a game of their own content.

Hopkins Humanitarian Charity Mine

This is the scenario used in the example of play section in the players guide.

What the Players Know:

The players have been sent by Hopkins and Oslin Astro-Mining to the Hopkins and Oslin Gravium Mine on CS-264, commonly called the "Hopkins Humanitarian Charity Mine," because the workers there complained about an unknown creature that has damaged their supplies. Hopkins and Oslin have sent the PCs to the facility to eliminate these creatures, assess profitability of the facility and, if the facility is found to be no longer profitable, liquidate all employees with extreme prejudice.

What the Players Don't Know:

This one is fairly straight forward. Depending on the alien, it is hiding in pockets of the asteroids that were exposed when the mining started.

Act 1:

Entering the facility, they can enter at either end and are talked in by the appropriate security guard. After a brief decontamination in the hanger they are greeted by the appropriate security guard, Jay Garrick and Nigel Brant, who brief them on what they know. Throw some bones here, but make sure they don't get a complete picture of the alien. An important thing to make sure of is that no one knows how the alien is getting through and around the facility. It is also explained that, due to the remoteness of the mine, any contact with corporate takes about 3 days to get a reply. Going down into the mine can lead to a confrontation with the alien, where they encounter it and it goes and hides somewhere. Keeping an eye on the security cameras will also lead to the players getting a look at the aliens.

Act 2:
Once the players have seen or encountered the alien they will probably try and find a way to kill it. This means going down into the mine. The mine is dark and has a number of easy to miss alcoves and side passages for the alien to ambush them. Going into the mine for a fight should be dangerous and if the players don't prepare, they will run into a lot of trouble. The most likely way for this act to end is for the players to find that the alien is using tunnels in the asteroid to get to parts of the facility, which should give them a good indication of how to deal with it.

Act 3:
Once the players know how the alien is getting around, they may determine that it's not worth it and try to leave. In this case, the miners and such will try and persuade them to stay or take them with them. Since leaving the facility without solving the problem would indicate a problem with profitability, you should encourage the players to kill the miners so they don't cause trouble. Of course, this would lead to it's own conflict. If they leave, have the alien sneak onto their ship and attack them when they think they are safe.

The Mining Facility:
There is no map for this scenario, but a description of the facility is still provided. The facility is broken into two wings, one above the mine shaft and one below. The top wing is where most of the living facilities and offices are. The security force, science personal and civilians live here. The bottom wing is more recent and smaller. The engineers live here.

Wing 1:
- **Cargo Bay 1:** Has whatever cargo was being carried. Has a security camera that reports to security room 1.
- **Science Lab:** Has equipment in it that gives +5 skill to

science checks while in that room. Has a security camera that reports to security room 1.
- **Cargo Bay 2:** Has whatever cargo was being carried. Has a security camera that reports to security room 1.
- **Bathroom 1:** Has a toilet and sink.
- **Bedrooms (3):** Has a bed. Has a security camera that reports to security room 1.
- **Armory 1:** Has 1 machine gun and 1 body armor
- Security Room 1: 10x10, has security cameras in 80% of the rooms which it can watch as well as the ability to lock doors to rooms with electric locks
- **Common Room:** Various tables, a microwave
- **Office:** Has a computer at the desk. Has a security camera that reports to security room 1.
- **Hanger 1:** Has a large outside door, can hold flying vehicles. Has a security camera that reports to security room 1.
- **Hallways (2):** Has a security camera that reports to security room 1.
- **Elevator Top:** Top of the elevator. Has x5 space suits. Has a security camera that reports to both security rooms.

Mine Shaft: (Between Wings)
- **Mine Shaft:** Goes down at an angle, it's dark in there
- **Furnace Room:** The heat is not enough to deal damage unless the furnace is damaged, in which case it deals 1 damage per round. This controls the heat and atmosphere of the facility
- **Elevator Middle:** Middle of the elevator. Has x5 space suits. Has a security camera that reports to both security rooms.

Wing 2:
- **Security Room 2:** Has security cameras in 80% of the rooms which it can watch as well as the ability to lock doors to rooms with electric locks
- **Courtyard:** A nice open space. Has a security camera

that reports to security room 2.
- **Cargo Bay 3:** Has whatever cargo was being carried. Has a security camera that reports to security room 2.
- **Bathroom 2:** Has a toilet and sink.
- **Supply Closets (2):** Has cleaning supplies
- **Armory 2:** Has 1 shotgun and 1 body armor. Has a security camera that reports to security room 2.
- **Bedroom:** Has a bed. Has a security camera that reports to security room 2.
- **Hanger 2:** Has a large outside door, can hold flying vehicles
- **Hallways:** Connects various rooms.
- **Elevator Bottom:** Bottom of elevator. Has x5 space suits. Has a security camera that reports to both security rooms.

NPCS:
Scientists:
- **Nigel Brant** (Head Scientist) - Theoretical Science
- **Trevor Seven** (Android) - Chemistry
- 2 other scientists

Soldiers:
- **Cat Castor** (Security, Wing 2) - Firearms
- **Dys Silver** (Security, Wing 1) - Firearms
- **Neon Skywalker** (Security, Shift) - Firearms

Engineers:
- **Beans Ferk** (Head Engineer) - Jury Rig
- **"Red"** - Mechanical
- 4 other engineers

Civilians:
- **Roger Simple** (Manager) - Social
- **Jay Garrick** (Secretary) - Social
- 5 other civilians

The Long Runner, a Commercial Freight Ship:

What the Players Know:
They are on a commercial ship transporting goods (food, replacement parts, etc) to a Terra-Firma Co. terraforming colony on Planet Andromida 518 along with a executive from Terra-Firma Co., Bert Porter.

What the Players Don't Know:
Bert Porter has hidden a dangerous alien created in a laboratory in the cargo bay at the request of Terra-Firma Co. in order to "discover a new life-form" on Andromida 518.

Act 1:
It starts with the players waking up from cryo-sleep and sitting down for a meal. Give the players some time to get introduced to the NPCs and the setting. After the meal either send one of the players or Lia out to the engine room to check on a low-priority problem where they find signs that might point to something alive being on the ship such as bite marks, fluids or the like. The specifics depend on the alien. While that's going on, get another player in communication with the terraforming colony for a basic update and to let everyone know that they'll be getting there in a couple days or so and everyone on the ship is out of cryo-sleep. The people on the colony will tell them to stay in contact daily. In a little bit, cut to people making dinner. Whoever is cooking finds that a good deal of the food is gone and the fridge open. (If the alien eats that is. If it doesn't, they find more signs on the alien in the kitchen) During dinner let them all talk about things so far. Don't draw too much suspicion towards Bert during this. Act 1 ends when a player or NPC is isolated and attacked. The med bay, cockpit and cargo bay are good places for this. If an NPC is attacked, the players find bits of his corpse to end act 1.

Act 2:
The alien will act according to it's behaviors, but it should be active enough where the players don't feel like they can wait it out and let the colonists handle it. If the alien can make use of the vents it should. Bert should act increasingly suspiciously through the act and will try to keep the alien alive in a low-key manner. Even if they figure out that he's the one who brought the alien he keeps his loyalty to the company and figures he can wait things out and kill the people that know the alien isn't native to the planet with poison or by tricking them into being alone with the alien.

Act 3:
Whatever the players come up with to kill the alien, Bert will sabotage if he can. He'll go pretty far, even risking the safety of core parts of the ship if it gets the job done. If the players are planning to run away, he'll launch the escape pods before they can get to them. If there are multiple smaller aliens or one is captured, he'll try to hide it in a cryo pod for safe keeping or launch it to the planet in an escape pod.

Rooms:
1. **Common Room** - The most furnished room on the ship. Has a dinner table, a couch and fold out beds.
2. **Cockpit** - Filled with the controls of the ship.
3. **Engine Room** - Fairly well maintained, this room is cluttered with various machinery.
4. **Kitchen** - A typical kitchen.
5. **Bathroom** - It has a toilet, shower and a sink. It's pretty cramped.
6. **Med Bay** - This room is very clean and has medical supplies and devices arranged neatly throughout.
7. **Cargo Bay** - This large room is full of boxes. Most contain replacement parts but some have food, letters or other personal requests from the colonists.
8. **Cryo Bay** - This room is empty aside from a computer

unit and the cryo-beds that it controls.
9. **Hallway** - A hallway.
10. **Escape Pods** - This room has 4 pods for 1 person each.
11. **Airlock** - This room has 2 heavy doors on both the exit and entrance to keep the ship properly sealed.
12. **Vents** - Not on the map. These vents could fit a medium sized dog if one tried to crawl through them.

NPCs:
- **Dr. Timothy Hectos** - Surgery. A quiet doctor. He goes by Tim.
- **Lia Knoff** - Mechanical. The ship's engineer. She doesn't take her work very seriously.
- **Bert Porter** - Social. An executive for Terra-Firma Co. He's friendly, but that's just at face value.

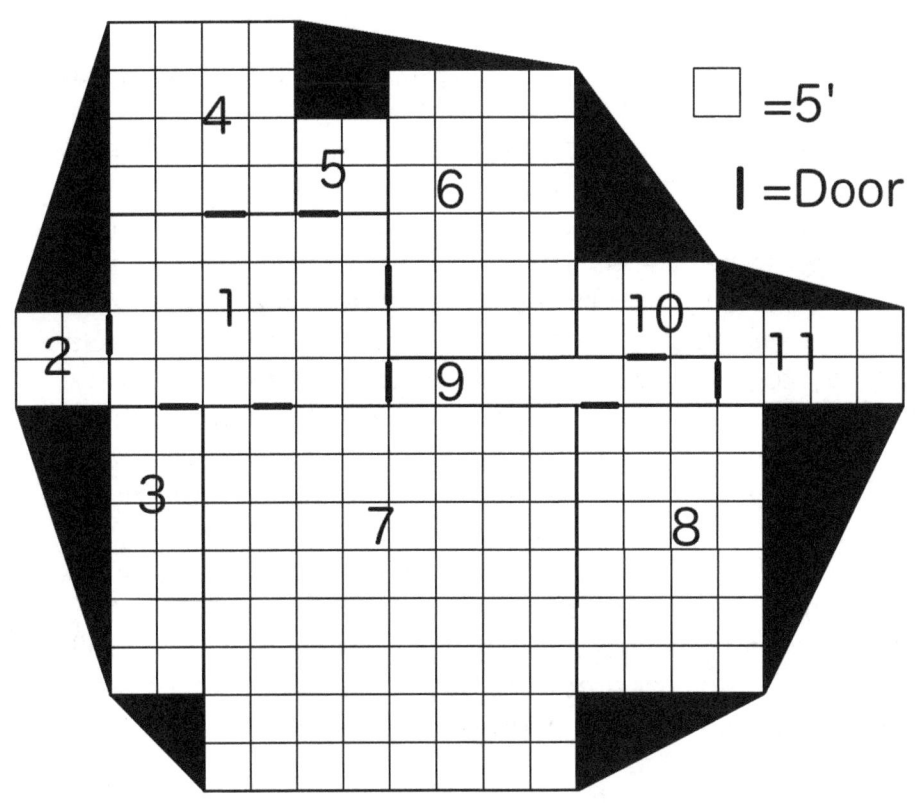

Mayall Planet-216:

What the Players Know:
They've just crashed their ship on Mayall 216, a highly irradiated rock out in the middle of a hyperspace route where no one would ever pass going slower than light. They've set up a distress beacon, but who knows when or if someone will hear it.

What the Players Don't Know:
There is a dangerous creature that lives on the planet, hibernating for centuries and only leaving hibernation to hunt for food that falls to the planet. The crash of the player's ship woke it up and it is headed to their location looking for a meal.

Act 1:
The players will likely try to stay at their ship since it is safer than going outside into the desert. While the players have a distress beacon, it will be about a month before they get a response so they'll probably need to do more than just wait. They probably don't have a full amount of space-suits or other protection so expect them to want to stay put no matter what happens. Through most of this act, the alien is scoping the ship out from a distance and mainly makes it's moves at night, since the darkness will better hide it. Use this part to build suspense and make sure to never show the alien in it's entirety. Start by having them find tracks or scratches, then work up to shapes in the darkness and seeing individual features, such as a tail, as the creature is moving out of sight. The players will likely be putting up watches. If they are, end the act with the alien attacking the person on watch 3 or 4 nights in. If they don't put up a watch, the alien attacks them when they sleep. This will likely kill multiple characters, but don't tone it down since they really should have been more careful.

Act 2:
The alien will probably try to lure them out of the ship, but is somewhat content to wait them out while they start to starve. Emphasize their supplies going low and make sure they know that starvation is an issue. If the players start setting up traps, this is a good thing. If they venture out to the bunker in search of food or other supplies, the alien will try and trap them in the bunker and wait them out even more. If the group splits with some people going to the bunker, it stays with the smaller group. The alien knows that there is no help on the planet and is fine with people splitting off from the main group since it can hunt them down later.

Act 3:
This act has a couple of ways to start, either the players have waited a month and gotten a reply that help is on the way or they have harvested parts from the bunker and are repairing their ship. If help is on the way it will take another 2 weeks, but the alien has noticed the change in their spirits and becomes more aggressive. If they are repairing their ship they will have to work on the outside of the ship, which the alien notices and takes advantage of when it can. Either way, the alien sees that something is up and realize it can't just wait for them to get weak from hunger.

Areas:
- **The Planet** - Mayall 216 is primarily a rocky radioactive desert, though it does have some bizarre jungles of radiation-eating plants at it's poles. While it does have a breathable atmosphere, there is no magnetic sphere which is why the planet is so heavily irradiated while outside. The radiation deals 1 damage per hour to anyone not wearing some sort of protective gear. Androids and the alien do not take this damage. The players start in their crashed ship with a distress beacon which they've probably already set up. Out in the distance there is a small bunker structure which has a number of skeletons of some sort of unknown, but apparently intelligent aliens.

There are signs of struggle and all the equipment is broken. Parts can be salvaged for the player's ship, but this takes several days and the parts are heavy enough to count as 4 items. Other features of the planet are a set of cliffs and a dried out river which show up if the players explore beyond just checking out the bunker.

- **Crashed Ship** - The players ship. It is heavily damaged and incapable of flight. Most of the rooms are damaged and have hull breaches that let in radiation. The only undamaged rooms are the cockpit, kitchen and airlock.
- **Bunker** - A small but visible metal structure with a door that is stuck partly open. Inside there are a number of skeletons of some sort of unknown, but apparently intelligent aliens as noted by the advanced technology of the building. There are signs of struggle and all the equipment is broken. Parts can be salvaged for the player's ship, but this takes several days and the parts are heavy enough to count as 3 items per part. The players need 5 parts to fix their ship. The bunker is about 1/2 a days walk from the crashed ship.
- **Cliffs** - Rocky cliffs that drop off a few hundred feet, enough to kill pretty much anything that falls. There isn't really anything here to help the players, but it might help to have the terrain at their back. A full day's walk from the crashed ship, 1/2 a days walk from the bunker.
- **Dry River** - A dried out river bed. There are some plants growing here, but only enough to feed 3 people for a day. A full day's walk from the crashed ship and a day and a half's walk from the bunker.

Exo-Colony "Pleasantsville:"

What the Players Know:
The players have been sent to Pleasantsville by the government of Earth because there has been no communication with the colony for nearly 2 months. The government suspects that they are staging some sort of rebellion and that this is their declaration of independence. They are to try and figure out what happened and send a report back. They are not to take any violent action against the colonists, but just to warn them that any rebellion will have consequences.

What the Players Don't Know:
The colonists have been almost entirely wiped out by the alien. While the colonists had encountered and even started to domesticate the known life on the planet, the apex predator wasn't discovered until it found them. Most of the facility has signs of the alien having been there, but it is all circumstantial.

Act 1:
Most of this should be the players trying to piece together what happened to the colony. Throw clues about the alien's traits and features but don't have the alien actually appear. The players should be able to figure out approximations of what most of the traits are, but leave at least one as a surprise. When they get back to their ship, it is damaged enough where it doesn't fly. After this, the players will probably send their report back with what they think happened, use this to ambush them partway through.

Act 2:
The players will probably ask for help in their report, but the communication is one way so they don't know how long it will take. The best that they have is an estimate of one week. Sitting tight might seem like their best bet and they

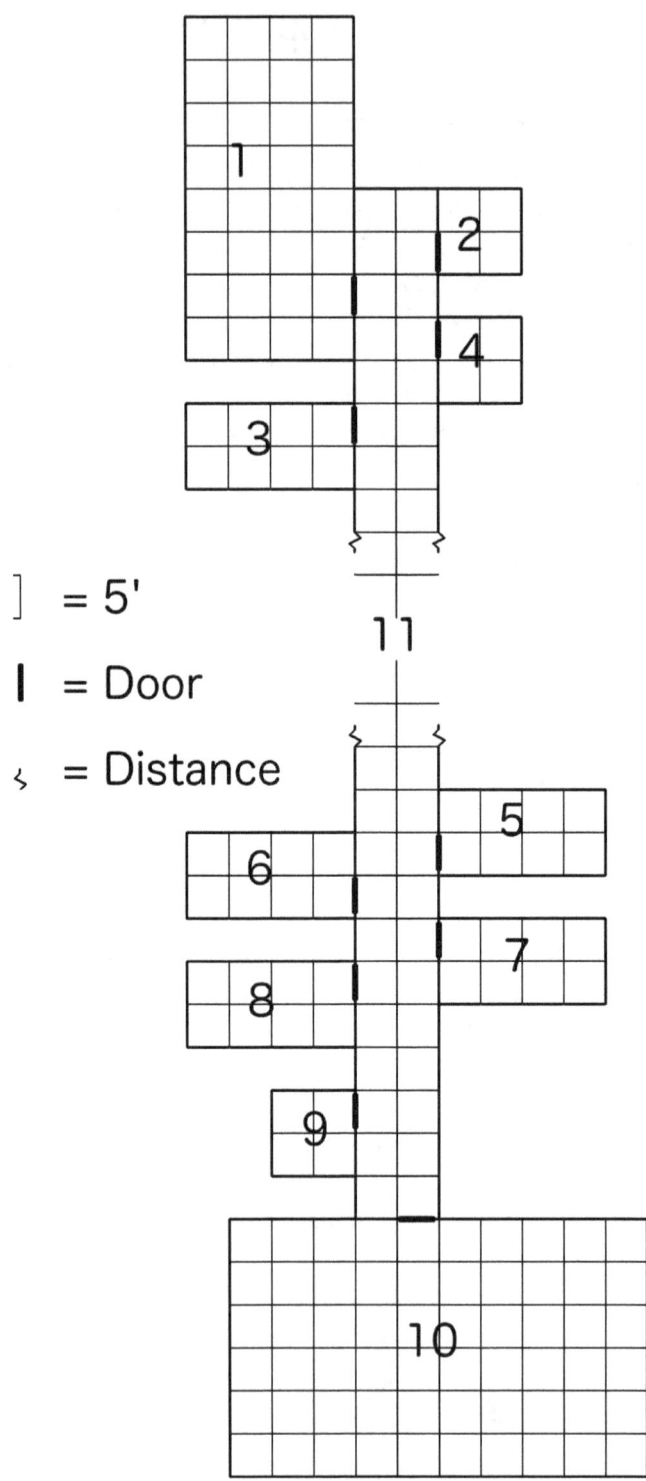

] = 5'

| = Door

≶ = Distance

132

will probably fortify their ship as they work on it or a relatively secure room. Throw the players off by having some survivors show up either on a security camera or outside the room the players are holed up in. They'll tell the players more about the alien, but only if they let them in. Play it up as a moral crisis since these people are terrified. The alien isn't scared of the players unless it has reason to be, so make sure that they feel trapped wherever they are.

Act 3:
There really isn't a concrete way that this act opens, but if the players waited for help to arrive, they are massacred unless the players were waiting in the hanger or otherwise at the landing sight when it arrives. Even in this case, have the alien go on full offense and really tear things up. If this damages the rescue ship, everyone will likely die. This is fine. If the players go after the alien, then it should be a tough fight even if they get the drop on it. This thing managed to take out an entire colony on it's own anyway.

Rooms:
Wing 1:
1   **Bathroom:** A mundane bathroom.
2   **Barracks:** Contains rows of bunkbeds with lockers at the feet. Most of the lockers are full of personal affects, but one of them contains a pistol.
3   **Bedroom:** A mundane bedroom.
4   **Trash Disposal:** A large furnace for disposing of trash
5   **Sewers:** Not listed on the map. A series of tunnels with a few feet of refuse filled water. Connects up with bathrooms and other sewers.
Wing 2:
6   **Bedroom x4:** A mundane bedroom.
7   **Security Room:** A small room with a bank of computer monitors that can view all hallways, the hanger and the barracks.
8   **Hanger:** A large, mostly empty room. A power mover

is in one of the corners

11   **Vents:** Not listed on the map. A series of small tunnels that could fit a large dog inside of them connecting to every room in the complex aside from the sewers.

5   **Sewers:** Not listed on the map. A series of tunnels with a few feet of refuse filled water. Connects up with bathrooms and other sewers.

NPCs: 0 living, 102 dead colonists

CHAPTER 10: Sample Worlds

Sample World Details:
The samples listed here are meant not only for quick start, but also for filling in details or keeping consistency across multiple games. They focus on technology and where humanity is in it's development. Most of these work best by mixing them together.

Corporate Future:
International or interplanetary corporations own everything. All travel, faster than light or otherwise, is controlled by corporations who only use it for their own gain. People may or may not have barcode tattoos, but androids definitely do. Humans are treated like comodities and if they are costing the company money they are more than happy to have them killed. The players are probably working to pay off some sort of debt or otherwise coerced into whatever they are doing when the aliens show up.

Grunge Future:
Earth is no longer the only planet with human civilization, but most of the technology that got them to that point hasn't filtered down to the general public. Most people live in cramped living conditions eating nutrient pills and generally being unhappy. Faster than light technology may or may not exist, but if it does it should be too expensive for anyone less than a CEO or government official. Androids are probably nearly indistinguishable from humans, but rare. Since most games are set somewhere in space, the players are probably just doing their jobs when the aliens show up or they are some kind of government taskforce tasked with some kind of dangerous bug-hunt.

Utopian Future:
Things are looking up. Food, healthcare and housing are avaible to all and because of the unity humanity has found

within itself has led to incredible advances in technology. Most work is either voluntary or automated and the quality of life for the average person is very high. Androids are treated with full citizen ship and have been allowed to develop their own cultures. What the players are doing is pretty open-ended given the relative freedom, but they may be part of a disaster relief crew, explorers or even vacationers.

Post-Apocalyptic:
Civilization is on the mend from some great disaster. The details of this disaster aren't overly important, but it likely isolated many planetary colonies from most of civilization leading to the formation of widely varying cultures. Technology from before the disaster is breaking down or lost and faster than light travel is a thing that is lost for the most part. The players likely are working to re-establish contact with former colonies and my come into conflict with them.

Near-Future:
Humanity has just started sending out the first ships to other solar systems. Faster than light travel has not yet been invented and the travel is either done via multi-generation ships or cryogenic sleep pods. If there are any androids, they are likely the first model of artificial humans and are very stiff in how they move, act and look. The players may be the first out-planet colonists, interselar explorers or any other type of pioneers into the unknown. Technology is comparable to what exists now, but different enough to feel futuristic

CHAPTER 11: Final Notes

Through reading this book, particularly part 3, you've likely noticed the relative informality of the aliens and scenarios. Since the players won't be looking at any of the "behind the scenes" content you generate for a game you should feel beholden to the exact numbers and abilities. In general, the game runs more smoothly and is more fun if you run things by what makes sense to happen rather than by stiffly adhering to the numbers. If the alien doesn't get the climb trait, but it would make for a really good scene to have the players find the alien by panning up a flashlight to the ceiling where the alien is waiting to drop down on them for an ambush, go for it. Even the example of gameplay in part 1 does this. If you look at the Gravoid sample alien and the Hopkins Oslin Charity Mine sample scenario don't work as the exact details would say. The mineshaft does not have an atmosphere in it, and this should kill the Gravoid since it does not have the "Can Live in Space" trait, but the Gravoid is unfazed because the game would be pretty boring if it just died whenever it tried to leave it's nest. Sure, that trait could have been added to the alien, but that's not really needed because it's an incidental detail. Be sure to keep the alien mostly consistent within a given game though, since the players will start to think that there isn't any rules to the game and that, as such, nothing in the game matters. After all you do put numbers to the alien for a reason, even if that reason is not the same as most tabletop games.

The more a group of people play the game the more they will be able to understand what the alien can do. While Alien Outbreak is designed to minimize this it is ultimately unavoidable. Here are a couple ideas of how to deal with this:
- Create new traits or other types of content for the alien and scenarios. This takes extra work and will only stave off the problem for a limited amount of time. It also might

lead to your players recognizing what you made as different from what was included in the base content of the book. That is not to say that content that you create will not be as good as the content of this book (In fact, since new content will be tailored towards a specific design rather than a list to be mixed and matched, your content will likely be more fitting to the way you and your group play the game.) but it may differ considerably from the design philosophy that this book was written under since that is not discussed in detail. The upside of this route is that creating new content whole-cloth will very directly solve the problem of keeping your players guessing.

- Start playing the game more like a traditional tabletop RPG with multiple sessions and consistent characters can work under the rules. You could easily do this by having recurring aliens for "sequels" to sessions every once in a while. The players will probably see this as another try at something they failed at or as the return of a cool thing that they overcame under different circumstances. In the case of the characters beating a session and having another of the same alien showing up for a later session, consider throwing a whole bunch of that alien at them for a challenge boost. You could also reuse a setting that was particularly memorable, such as a deadly planet or a facility that everyone died in. The downside is that it is very easy to meta-game the alien, since the characters being played may not have encountered the reused alien or setting. Longer campaigns don't run into that as much since the characters will be fairly consistent, and the game will gradually become more driven by the character's motivations and their relation to various NPCs. In this case, it is best to flesh out the world and characters that inhabit it more than you normally would and include sessions that don't focus on encounters with deadly aliens for changes in pacing.
- You can also play into the recognition. This is tricky since it walks a line between the mood aspect of the game and the "gamey" aspect of the game. Consider

throwing hints about how the game will play out, then subverting those hints. This method will likely burn out quickly, but could lead to an interesting meta-arms race between the GM and the players.

- There is also the option of handing the book off to someone else. This could either be to another member of your tabletop group, letting them GM for a while with you as a player for a change of perspective and probably a change of play style, or giving the book to a different group entirely. Every game is going to have a limit before people get sick of it and that is fine. This game is designed for people to have fun with and if you've played it to the point where it is no longer fun it has run it's course. Personally, if someone plays this game enough where they start to hate it I, the author, will be honored that, not only did you decide to play this game, but liked it enough where it reached that point.

Thanks for picking up this book. Hopefully you have fun playing Alien Outbreak with some friends at least a couple times and enjoy the rest of your day.

Game Master's Glossary

Acid - Deals damage to a character when submerged or splashed. Page 22

Actions - What a character can do. Page 14

Agility - A statistic that measures how well a character can control their physcial actions. Page 7

Alien - The main antagonist of the game. Page 40

Alien Description - A written physical description and introduction to the alien. Page 65

Android - A synthetic humanoid that players can pick as an alternative to being human. Page 9

Basic Attack - A generic attack that all aliens can use. Page 67

Behavior - A guideline for how the alien acts. Page 60

Civilian - A generalist kit that is weaker but can pick their options. Page 8

Cheating - Special abilities for the alien that change the rules of how it functions. Page 63

Combat - A more heavily metered section of play used for life or death situations. Page 14

Combat Round - A measure of all of the turns for each character once. Page 14

Combat Turn - A single character's actions during a combat round. Page 14

Collapse - What happens when heavy objects fall on a character. Page 22

Cold - Covers exposure to extreme cold. Page 22

Damage - A reduction to toughness as the result of Physical injury taken. Page 15

Death/Dying - A state that occurs when a character reaches 0 toughness. Page 16

Dice Notation - A system of shorthand for how many dice as well as what type to roll. Page 5

Dynamic Difficulty Score (Player) - A score kept by the game master that records how well or how poorly the players are doing. Page 20

Dynamic Difficulty Score (GM) - A measure of how well or poorly the players are doing. Page 79
Engineer - A kit focused on repairing or creating machines. Page 8
Equipment - A collection of carried items. Page 10
Falling - Deals damage when a character falls a long distance. Page 22
Fire - Deals damage to characters when exposed to it. Page 22
Game Master - The person running the alien, scenario and game at large. Page 3
Human - The default option for player characters. Page 9
Instinct - A statistic that affects the alien's attack rolls. Page 40
Intelligence - A statistic that measures a character's knowledge. Page 7
Item - An object that can be owned by a character. Page 10
Jumping - How far a character can leap. Page 22
Kits - A set of equipment, skill options and bonuses to certain statistics. Page 8
Layout - The way that rooms in the setting connect. Page 71
Morale - A statistic that measures how well a character can cope with stress and fear. Page 7
Morale Damage - A reduction to morale as the result of fear or other mental injury taken. Page 16
Panic - A state that occurs when a character reaches 0 morale. Page 16
Perception - A statistic that measures how attentive to detail and their surroundings a character is. Page 7
Player - All the people playing the game. Usually seperate from the game master. Page 3
Premise - The reason for the events of the game. Page 75
Radiation - Covers the effects of exposure to dangerous radiation. Page 23
Reproduction - An ability that determines how the alien reproduces. Page 61
Room - A space with certain traits or functions. Page 71

Scenario - The setting and reason that the players are dealing with through the game. Page 68
Scientist - A kit focused on intelligence and science. Page 8
Setting - The location in which the game takes place. Page 68
Size - Determines how large the alien is, as well as alterations to statistics and how much reach it has. Page 59
Skills - Areas of expertise that require training for proficiency. Page 18
Skill Check - A roll made on 3d10 against the skill bonus + 1/2 a statistic made to use a skill. Page 14
Skill Points - Points obtained during character creation that are added into skills as a bonus to that skill. Page 9
Smoke - Rules for the effects of smoke in combat. Page 23
Soldier - A kit focused on combat. Page 8
Special - A statistic that determines how often the alien can use certain traits. Page 40
Speed - A statistic that determines how fast the alien moves. Page 40
Statistics (Alien) - A measure of the alien's qualities. Page 40
Statistics (Player) - A measure of the qualities of a character. Page 6
Statistic Bonus - A bonus equal to 1/2 the statistic applied to skill rolls. Page 13
Statistic Check - A roll made on 3d10 against a statistic. Page 14
Strength (Alien) - A statistic that affects the alien's melee damage. Page 40
Strength (Player) - A statistic that measures the physical strength of a character. Page 6
Structure - Determines the number of limbs that the alien has. Page 59
Three Act Structure - A system of breaking the game into 3 sections that each have distinct traits to them. Page 78
Toughness (Alien) - A statistic that measures how much damage the alien can sustain. Page 40

Toughness (Player) - A statistic that measures how much damage a character can withstand. Page 7

Traits - The positive abilities the alien gets. Page 41

Underwater - Rules for when characters are submerged in fluid. Page 23

Vacuum - The vacuum of space. Extremely harmful. Page 23

Vehicles - Objects that can be piloted with the use of a vehicle key. Page 12

Weakness - The negative abilities the alien gets. Page 57

CPSIA information can be obtained
at www.ICGtesting.com
Printed in the USA
BVHW061531180319
542960BV00008B/448/P